The Roots of Our Faith

The Roots of Our Faith

Ancient Egypt And The Bible

James K. Ocansey, Ph.D.

Writers Club Press
San Jose New York Lincoln Shanghai

The Roots of Our Faith
Ancient Egypt And The Bible

All Rights Reserved © 2002 by James K. Ocansey

No part of this book may be reproduced or transmitted in any form or by any means, graphic, electronic, or mechanical, including photocopying, recording, taping, or by any information storage retrieval system, without the permission in writing from the publisher.

Writers Club Press
an imprint of iUniverse, Inc.

For information address:
iUniverse, Inc.
5220 S. 16th St., Suite 200
Lincoln, NE 68512
www.iuniverse.com

ISBN: 0-595-21474-6

Printed in the United States of America

Dedicated:

First, to the Lord Jesus Christ, Who said: "You shall know the Truth and the Truth shall make you free" (John8:32).

Second, to my wife Joyce Ama Ocansey of thirty years, who stood by my side all these years. Also to Martha, Christopher and Keni whose support have made this work possible.

Contents

FOREWORD ix
PREFACE xv
INTRODUCTION: THE ROOTS OF OUR FAITH 1
CHAPTER 1   THE STORY OF ANCIENT EGYPT 7
CHAPTER 2   GOD'S BLUEPRINT FOREVER SETTLED IN HEAVEN—THE ZODIAC 13
CHAPTER 3   THE ANCIENT EGYPTIANS' CONCEPT OF GOD AND OF SATAN 25
CHAPTER 4   THE ANCIENT EGYPTIANS' CONCEPT OF MAN 37
CHAPTER 5   THE DYNAMIC RELATIONSHIP BETWEEN GOD, SATAN AND MAN 43
CHAPTER 6   "I AM NOT COME TO DESTROY, BUT TO FULFIL" (Mt. 5:17b) 49
CHAPTER 7   ARE CHRISTIANS ASHAMED OF THEIR ROOTS? 61
CHAPTER 8   "I AM THE WAY, THE TRUTH AND THE LIFE" (John 14:6) 77
CHAPTER 9   SUMMARY, CONCLUSIONS, AND SOME IMPLICATIONS 85
EPILOGUE: WHEN WE SHUT OUT THE LIGHT 99

REFERENCES 103
About the Author 107

FOREWORD

At the beginning of the 21st Century when knowledge has exploded exponentially, and is available on the Internet both good and evil, it is tragic to observe that American public school students have been deprived of the only source of knowledge that counts. It is the only knowledge that will help them discern good from evil, right from wrong. It is the Word of God which says "The fear of the Lord is the beginning of wisdom" (Ps.111:10). They have been deprived of wisdom and the only source of Power, which can make a difference in their lives.

Spiritual and moral growth can have their foundation only in the absolute truths of God as established in the Bible, which has its deepest roots and the bedrock of its foundation in ancient Egypt. It is this connection that this study seeks to establish.

How this exclusion came about, for whose interests or for what motives is not the subject of this study. The concern is that it happened, and the triune God (the Father, Son and Holy Spirit) has been officially excluded from the knowledge of Public school children. As a result there has been a downward spiral in morality and in the development of children as quality human beings. This has resulted in children being exposed to the works of darkness which is easy to document in lack of self discipline, drug use, the feeling of hopelessness, and such manifestations as school shootings to destroy lives whose worth only the Bible helps us to appreciate. The Word of God says:

> "Professing to be wise, they became fools" (Rom.1:22), and "God gave them over to a debased mind, to do those things which are not fitting" (Rom.1:28).

The concern which this study seeks to draw attention to is that because of the exclusion of the Bible from our schools, whole areas of knowledge have been shut off from our children. This is in the area of revelation knowledge, which has been in existence since the dawn of history. It is direct knowledge from God through dreams, visions, ability to interpret dreams; miracle healing, word of knowledge and other gifts of the Spirit which only those in the Lord are equipped to understand. It also includes wisdom from the study of God's Word.

Scientific knowledge gained through empirical observation has no clue about revelation knowledge since the things of God are not physically observable. For instance, only the results of miracle healing can be observed but not how it happened. Many of these are everyday experiences in a Benny Hinn crusade, which some children view on TV every morning on "This is Your Day for a Miracle". People experience the Power of God flowing through their bodies and manifesting itself in the form of electricity or heat within the body and especially in the area of the body that is receiving healing. God's power also manifests itself in "word of knowledge" in which the presence of the Holy Spirit reveals knowledge past, present or future, to God's servant in ways that science has no inkling. These are but a few of the areas of knowledge which Public school children are deprived of as the Bible is excluded from their knowledge.

Revelation knowledge has been used by individuals who through dreams have found solutions to problems. Some of these led to great inventions or achievements. It has been said that Christopher Columbus depended on such truth revealed in scriptures as "when He drew a circle on the face of the deep" (Prov.8:27b) to believe that the world was round instead of flat. This encouraged him, through prayers, to be able to sail to the New World. The early God-believing scientists believed that they were only "thinking God's thoughts after Him". It is correctly claimed that true science only serves to prove that the Bible is true and not the other way round.

In Genesis we read that God revealed to Pharaoh in a dream what He was about to do. There would be great abundance for seven years, followed by seven years of famine. God used Joseph to interpret Pharaoh's dream, which led to his promotion to the position second only to Pharaoh himself. This in turn led to his whole family coming to settle in Egypt. This was how the Hebrews came to establish as a people in ancient Egypt for 430 years before their exodus when God showed Himself strong on their behalf in fulfillment of a promise He made to Abraham (Gen.15:13-14). This shows their roots from ancient Egypt but the fact that many fail to admit is that the very ideas and concepts they developed of God were actually in existence long before they even came there. The concept of monotheism was promoted by Pharaoh Akhanaton who attempted to establish it during his lifetime. It was, however, squashed soon after his death. This and many other ideas were in existence and formed the context in which the Hebrew people emerged. Here too was mapped the Zodiac with "the Seed of the woman" being established as Jesus to destroy the works of Satan.

Jesus came to fulfill ancient prophecies that dated back to the blueprint that had been established in the heavens, and He is the reason for our present millenium.

This work attempts to trace the roots of the Christian faith to ancient Egypt. Even though this should be obvious, it appears to be deliberately cut off from the knowledge of many of the people of God. It appears that Satan has used racial prejudice, especially in America, to deny the African connection of the values and teachings found in the Old Testament such as are found in the "Ten Commandments". Because the Bible is excluded from the knowledge of our Public school children, not only the fact of the African connection, but also the knowledge and the wisdom of God are excluded from them. The Bible says that wisdom is the principal thing and advises one to get wisdom and not to lean on one's own understanding. When Saul became Paul, he exchanged the wisdom of the world for the wisdom of God and claimed that his former Jewish faith and knowledge was like garbage compared to his new found faith and the treasures of wisdom found in Jesus Christ (Phil.3:1-11).

Children who have been cut off from the study of the Bible in school are not only shut off from the light; they become effectively exposed to darkness. This is the concern that this study is voicing so that American Public school education at the beginning of the 21st century will reconsider the irreparable damage not only to the children but to the whole society. What spiritual values will inform and direct the decision-making process in the technological breakthroughs such as on the Internet? Will children be helped to understand that there is a Higher Power above all powers, the Power that raised Jesus from the dead and that God Almighty is still at work, and that He is the source of love, joy and peace regardless of one's situation in life? How long will the truth of God be withheld from them?

It is my prayer that this study will draw attention to some of the issues Education policy makers need to be concerned about.

James Kwaku Ocansey.

ACKNOWLEDGMENTS

I owe a debt of gratitude first to the Almighty God for enabling me put together this study, which has long been in incubation and in the process of maturing. As an educator, my concern is basically the type of education that will not only help students make a living. It is also that which will enable them become successful human beings. This can only be found in the Word of God.

I have been exposed to the Bible through many teachers of the Word and it is practically impossible for me to mention all but a few. These include Kenneth Hagin, and the late Dr. Robert A Cook of Family Radio. The late Dr. Richard Helverson, chaplain of the United States Senate for a number of years, has been a long time favorite radio teacher with his wisdom in applying the Word of God to day-to-day situations. Others include Kenneth Copeland, Creflo Dollar Jr. and many other charismatic teachers of the Word.

In addition to the above, I have found many programs on the TV from which I have learned so much. Dr. D. James Kennedy had a series of messages on "The Real Meaning of the Zodiac" (later published) which inspired this study. I have also found the contributions of Prof. Yosef Ben-Jochannan and Prof. Charles S. Finch in Afrikan Origins of The Major World Religions of great help in this study. Above all, I am greatly indebted to Pastor Benny Hinn, considered by many, to be the world's number one evangelist today, greatly anointed by God to take the gospel literally to all the nations of the world. As a partner, I not only watch his program every morning, and tape it for my wife to watch; I also study from the teaching tapes he releases from time to time. After this study was almost completed, he released a study on tape entitled: "War in the Heavenlies". I found that it confirmed much that was discussed in this study and I also made references to it.

Reference has also been made to Dr. Cameron's book: The last Pew on the Left: America's lost potential, which has identified racism and racist attitudes both within and outside the Church as having done a great deal of damage to the United States of America in lost potential. To him I owe a debt of gratitude.

To my friends and colleagues who took time to read through and offer their comments, I am highly grateful. I must single out Mrs. Gifty Kusi who was the first to give me her comments. I also owe a debt of gratitude to Dr. Kofi Afriyie who has taken time out of his very busy schedule, to proofread and offer useful comments.

I am also indebted to my lovely wife, Joyce, of thirty years, for her encouragement in all my years of study at Columbia. To my adult sons and daughter on whom I called whenever I got stuck on the computer, I say "Thank you". Special "thanks" goes to Keni for his work in designing the front and back cover of this book. Above all, I thank Mrs. Aldred, the widow of the late Cyril Aldred, for permission to use for the front cover, the picture of the Pyramid of King Kheops with the Great sphinx at Giza.

My prayer is that this work will bring understanding to many of God's children while at the same time open the eyes of those who consider Christianity a "Western Religion" and reject it on that score. My prayer is also that it would speak to education policy makers of this nation about the greatest injustice to our Public School children when we exclude from them the light and knowledge of God. The Bible says: "Wisdom is the principal thing; Therefore get wisdom. And in all your getting, get understanding" (Pov.4:7). We forfeit both knowledge and wisdom without the study of the Word. Reference has already been made to the fear of God as the beginning of wisdom. In addition, the lost potential as a result of not teaching the Word of God in the public schools in America, is incalculable.

James K. Ocansey.

PREFACE

"My people are destroyed for lack of knowledge" (Hosea 4:6).
"And you shall know the truth, and the truth shall make you free" (John 8:32).

Ignorance of the Word of God is destructive because we are unaware of the fact that we are in a battle with Satan. We can only appropriate God's power that He makes available to us as believers when we stand on His Word. It is only the truth we know which can set us free. Many of God's people remain in mental bondage because of lack of information in some areas of the Word of God. This kind of bondage some one has called "an invisible force" which controls our lives and reactions. One area of bondage in America is that of race and racism which, as an invisible force, one may not even be aware of. It simply controls our thinking, feeling and reactions. Even the question of this study could generate a negative feeling or reaction in somebody under this kind of bondage. But open mindedness to seek after the truth according to the Word of God can bring us release from that bondage. As Christians, are we willing to seek after truth, or would we rather feel comfortable accepting the lies of the enemy? It is my prayer that this study will open the eyes of believers to the truth of the roots of their faith.

The question is: "Is the Christian religion Western or African in origin?" There are those in Africa and many of African descent who reject the Bible and Christianity as a Western religion because of its association with slavery and colonialism. It is therefore viewed as a religion of the oppressor. It is the purpose of this study to establish that Christianity, with the Bible, has its deep roots in ancient Egypt and that Africa was indeed the birthplace of Christianity.

There are also those who reject the Bible on philosophical grounds. By this is meant that some Evolutionist scientists who claim billions of years for the world conflict with Creation scientists who claim a young age. The latter claim that the world is six thousand years old. This study finds a ground for reconciliation for the two parties. This allows God to be the Creator while conceding to the position of billions of years for the Evolutionist scientists.

My chief purpose, however, is to establish that if indeed Christianity and the Bible has its roots in ancient Egypt, to reject the Bible in our Public school education system is to reject a source of knowledge whose roots date back to the cradle of civilization. What if we finally come to recognize that there is no conflict between the claims of science and the Bible, and that science is actually "thinking God's thoughts after Him" as stated by the founders of science?

It will be established that the roots of Christianity link us to ancient Egyptian developments in their understanding of who God is, as well as God as the Creator of the world and all that is in it. The laborious mapping of the heavens in what is called the Zodiac establishes God's blueprint for the world with Jesus, the Seed of the woman, being shown as the conqueror over Satan right from the beginning.

After this study was almost completed, a great man of God and teacher of the Word, released a study to the body of Christ. This study, I believe, to be very timely and relevant to this work because it provides a better environment for Christians to renew their minds with reference to the claims made in this work. The person is the well-known world evangelist Pastor Benny Hinn. The study was entitled: "War in the Heavenlies" and it was his more accurate translation of the Hebrew: "In the beginning" as "In the dateless past" which is of considerable interest to this study.

According to him, this dateless past, happened between Genesis 1:1 and 1:2. During this period, something happened to God's perfect creation. Isaiah says God did not create the world to be a "worthless waste" but to be inhabited (Is.45:18). Deuteronomy (32:4) also states that God created everything perfect. What happened was a destruction of God's perfect creation which He restored, starting from Genesis 1:3, when He said "Let there be light"…The word "let" is permission and not creation. This "dateless past", according to Pastor Benny, could be billions of years which covers what is called the pre-Adamic period. The destruction was caused by Lucifer's rebellion against God, which resulted in his being cast out of heaven. In the process, there was a catastrophic destruction of God's perfect creation as Lucifer who became Satan, pulled a third of the angels with him. These also became devils and demons that became chained in the pit or hell, but some still found themselves loose on earth.

We understand that this rebellion resulted in God moving the mountains out of place and overturning them in anger. The sun was commanded not to shine and the stars were sealed off while the world was covered with water (Job 9:5-8). We read: "He is the Maker of the Bear and Orion, the Pleiades and the constellations of the south" (Job 9:9), which the ancient Egyptians mapped out as the Zodiac.

It is stated that there was a sudden freezing of the waters after the sun refused to shine and the earth became a ball of ice in space. This sudden freezing caused an immediate destruction of life during the period science calls the ice-age when, among others, dinosaurs described in detail in Job (38-39) were also frozen to death.

All this then means that long before the theory of Evolution attempted to explain the world without God, we find that God not only created it but also had it all recorded in the Bible. Their assertion that the world could be billions of years is accounted for when we more accurately translate "In the beginning" as "In the dateless past…". But to assert that the world and life came into being by accident is definitely mistaken. Similarly, Creation scientists' claim of a young age of six thousand years for the world does not seem to have much basis. If that were so, it would make senseless such studies by archeologists of the many developments in ancient Egypt and such findings that prior to 25,000 BC the Sahara desert supported life, or that there were developments by 5,000 BC in ancient Egypt.

The claims of Evolutionist scientists and Creation scientists are therefore reconciled by this more accurate translation of "In the beginning" as "In the dateless past…".

It is said that the Bible interprets the Bible. This is because it is a library of sixty-six books written by thirty-five authors (from peasants to kings) in Hebrew, Aramaic and Greek, over about 1600 years (Hinckley, 1989:74). But it has an amazing unity and internal consistency in this diversity because the Holy Spirit inspired every writer and was actually the author. He revealed things in the past through visions concerning creation. It was so for Job, considered the oldest book in the Bible. Job (9:4-10) describes how God removed the mountains and overturned them in anger during Lucifer's rebellion, as well as God's creation of the constellations. Similarly we find the Holy Spirit inspiring Isaiah (14:4-21 and 24:1-5), as well as Jeremiah (4:23-27) and Ezekiel (28:13-19) as they each described Lucifer's rebellion and its consequences of wasteland from what God created to be perfect. They also point out not only Lucifer's defeat, but how God "did not make a full end" but decided to restore the world once more from its pre-Adamic flood.

This is the kind of revelation knowledge, which only God makes available of not only the past but also of the future. What does science know of revelation knowledge? What does it know of the numerous miracles that occur every day as God reveals to His servants through visions and dreams and "word of knowledge" not only what happened in the past but what will happen in the future?

We also know that if prophecy is from God, it is expected to be fulfilled with 100% accuracy, or the prophet is considered false. Prophecy in the Bible has been consistently fulfilled with 100% accuracy which is proof that they came from God. Here too we can say with confidence that science knows nothing of prophecy.

In this study, The roots of our Faith: Ancient Egypt and the Bible, there is confirmation that as the place of first claim to civilization, and the home of the Hebrews for 430 years, it indeed became the source and origin of much that we find in the Bible. It is believed that the garden of Eden described in Genesis 2:8-15, extended from Ethiopia north to Egypt, extending as far East as Iran. Ancient Egypt therefore would appear to be the most likely place that not only nourished the Christian faith, but was also the original source of much of the material we find in the Bible. God indeed revealed Himself to them, and our understanding of who God Almighty is has never changed much over time. Jesus came to fulfill the laws and the prophets and His disclosure of Himself is the only addition that supercedes everything else. He came to fulfill and not to destroy.

To jettison the Truth of God in the Bible is to reject the basic foundation of knowledge and so to expose students to the lies of Satan and to remove them from the kingdom of God into the kingdom of Satan with all its destructive consequences. This is especially so when a whole nation rejects God from its knowledge and allows only the lies of the enemy to be taught in its Public schools.

Truth cannot be sought from lies. By this is meant that the Evolutionary paradigm based on the deception of Satan, cannot provide a framework for attaining truth. As an educator, and a Christian convinced of the Truth of God, it is my great concern that great injustice is being done to our youth as a result of ignorance and prejudice concerning the Word of God. The injustice is that students are cut off from plugging into the Power of God through faith in Jesus Christ. It was this same Power that raised Jesus from the dead. It is the same power that is manifested in miracles, healing, and word of knowledge when the Holy Spirit is present.

Many problems in this, or in any other society at the individual or societal level, where the Truth and Power of God are not recognized, can be traced to the rejection of the Truth of God from their knowledge. It is my fervent prayer that believers as well as unbelievers will come to the knowledge of the Truth to set them free. More especially, those who have rejected the gospel because of a misconception of its origin, or have rejected it as a result of claims for a young age by some Christians, will be convinced to see that the truth of creation has long been recorded in the Bible. Science only attempts to understand what has long been settled in heaven.

INTRODUCTION: THE ROOTS OF OUR FAITH.

By "the roots of our faith" we mean the background or solid foundation provided for the Christian faith, which is a personal relationship with Jesus Christ. How relevant to this faith is ancient Egypt? It will be established in this study that the roots of Christian faith or belief in Jesus Christ go as far back as ancient Egypt. And why is this important to know? Why is this important to the average person whose faith might even be different?

The relevance is in the fact that everyone has a need or needs they want solved, regardless of the faith they hold. Some of these needs relate to daily living experiences in the face of the feeling of hopelessness all around us. It even might be how to respond to a destructive emotion; how to relate to one another or how to experience peace in one's heart in the face of turmoil. It all boils down to living successfully regardless of poverty or material wealth which does not necessarily translate into love, joy and peace of mind.

As an educator with over thirty years experience, and over twenty years in the New York City Public school system, my conviction is that there is a gaping need in the kind of education provided for our children and that needed for successful living. This is because of the exclusion of the Word of God from their knowledge. Many are unable to react responsibly to the daily challenges of life. As someone has put it, they are taught how to make a living but not how to live. In other words, making a living involves only the skills we employ on our jobs. To live life successfully goes beyond how much we earn. The educational experience leaves out much to be desired in the total education of body, mind and spirit. While body and mind are richly and profusely catered to, there is no similar balance in the education of the spirit which is totally ignored with the assumption that children will make correct choices in life. We are surprised when they make choices that are devoid of morality and suffer the consequences thereof. Spiritual laws are disregarded; correct responses in relating to people of other color, made in the image of God, are rare and devoid of respect and human dignity. Reactions stemming from a deep-seated feeling of racism were demonstrated when a group of four white policemen pumped forty-one bullets into a black person they immediately associated with a criminal. This suggests to me that the spiritual aspect of their education is lacking. It was the founder of the Christian faith that said: "It is the Spirit that gives life; the flesh profits nothing" (John 6:63), and yet the human spirit has been totally ignored in the educational process.

Another question one might ask is how relevant is ancient Egypt to all this? Such relevance is found in the fact that, as the cradle of civilization, Egypt was the place whose savant astronomer-priests not only mapped out the Zodiac but also detected the attributes of God in the heavenly bodies and stars. Christ and His subsequent work against Satan, recorded in the Bible, was first mapped out in the Zodiac which we will discuss later in more detail. The Bible which provides the basis of teachings on morality and human dignity has been taken out of the knowledge of our public school children, hence the spiritual laws and human relationships that stem from a relationship with God have been denied them. Paul writes in Romans 1:20:

> For since the creation of the world, His invisible attributes are clearly seen being understood by the things that are made, even His eternal power and Godhead, so that they are without excuse..."

Astronomy which is the science that deals with the origin, size, motion etc of the stars and planets, was used by the savant astronomer-priests to laboriously map out the heavens in what came to be known as the Zodiac. In those heavenly bodies, they detected the invisible attributes of God. But soon, Astronomy was superceded by Astrology which is defined as "the art of predicting or determining the influence of the planets and stars on human affairs." This was a distortion characteristic of Satan, the deceiver, where the "signs" put in the heavens to direct and focus attention on God, "the gospel in the stars", were actually prostituted to mean their influence on human affairs.

But why would it benefit anybody to know the truth about the real meaning of the Zodiac? The obvious reason is: "My people perish for lack of knowledge", according to Hosea (4:6). Decisions are often made based on astrological misdirection, and not on God's Truth. People often follow religious leaders because of lack of information. In this connection, it is refreshing to know that only one name has been established from the foundation of the universe, and that name is Jesus Christ. As will be discussed later, in all the "mansions" or "houses" of the Zodiac, Jesus Christ has been established as the conqueror over Satan.

The second reason why it is important to know and focus on Jesus and His work of redemption is that Bible prophecy seems to indicate that time is winding down and that His return is imminent. Taurus, the rampaging bull is soon to appear with judgement upon a sinful world. It matters little whether one believes it or not; that does not change God's sovereign overrule.

More important still, as far as education is concerned, is the chunk of knowledge that is left out when one ignores revelation knowledge. How can an industry that seeks knowledge and truth disregard a whole field of knowledge that is the source of wisdom and understanding derived from God the Creator? This is the only kind of knowledge not dependent on formal education but is neither limited to the non-formally educated. Despite the education of Moses and his preparation to become the next Pharaoh of Egypt, he would have continued as a fugitive from the law if God had not called him and endowed him with His Power. With that Power or anointing, he became the greatest leader through whom God brought out the Hebrews from Egypt through many miracles.

The apostle Paul, one of the most brilliant in his day, was exposed to that kind of knowledge when he met the Lord on the way to Damascus to persecute the Christians. He became the most outstanding apostle who wrote most of the New Testament books and Letters. That Power is still available to all. To the extent that our children are deprived of the knowledge of God, to that extent they are rendered impotent in achieving their highest potential in life. They are cut off from volumes of knowledge which science cannot provide nor explain. Empirical knowledge is based on what can be observed and measured but not so revelation knowledge which has no limits in time or space.

It is often said that the "anointing makes the difference". This is the Power of God which turns the ordinary person into an extraordinary one, or the natural into the supernatural. The highest potential God has for man can never be achieved without this anointing. Jesus Himself, the Son of God, had to have this anointing in order to do His work, and how much more does an ordinary person need it to reach his highest potential? Isaiah 61:1 fulfilled in Jesus states:

> The Lord has anointed Me to preach good tidings to the poor;
> He has sent Me to heal the brokenhearted,
> To proclaim liberty to the captives
> And the opening of the prison to those who are bound;...

It was the anointing which made everything possible for Him, and it is the same power that makes a difference in peoples' lives today. Our children go through a whole process of education with no idea of the source of the greatest power on earth which science, based on the principles of evolution, has no clue about.

Any education which disregards or intentionally deprives children of such knowledge is criminal, to say the least. Children are condemned to operate only in darkness and not in the light. Paul says of such: "Professing to be wise, they became fools" (Rom.1:22). It is the greatest injustice that can be done to students when they are deliberately deprived of the only kind of knowledge that can bring out the best in them.

There is one more area where the exclusion of the Bible from the knowledge of students is a great injustice. It relates to the fact that it also brings out the contributions in values and concepts developed in the Nile Valley in ancient Egypt, the source of much of what has been credited to Greece (James, 1988). Although that is not the main point of this study, it is suggested that racial pride has sought to exclude the positive aspects of ancient Egyptian contributions to what we find in the Bible. God's judgement on them, was not because of God's disfavor with them as a people, even though Exodus 11:7b tells us that "the Lord makes a difference between the Egyptians and Israel".

It is difficult for many to accept that God is no respecter of persons when He obviously sided with the Israelites against the Egyptians and later against the Canaanites. It was not all because they were held in slavery, nor was it because they were any more obedient to God. Despite everything that God did for them they continued to be rebellious and "stiff necked" and on more than one occasion, God almost wiped them out. At one time in the wilderness, they almost chose leaders to return them to Egypt (Num. 14:4). They were punished to wander in the wilderness for forty years until those over twenty died off because they refused Joshua and Caleb's report to go and possess the land God swore to their fathers (Num.14:23). How was it that God still seemed to be on their side?

It was because of God's blood-covenant with Abraham and his descendants to bless them and make them a blessing to the world (Gen.12:1-9). It was also that God desired a people for Himself through whom the Seed of the woman, Jesus Christ, would come. But above all, it seems that the main reason the Egyptians were punished was not because God was a respecter of persons. It was because their leadership, through Pharaoh, sided with Satan with whom God was and is at war. He said, "against all the gods of Egypt I will execute judgement: I am the Lord" (Ex 12:12). Judgement came on them because the leadership sided with Satan who first initiated war against God and had to be dealt with. Similarly, His judgement today is not based on color or race. It is based on whose side one is—God's or Satan's.

It is the Zodiac that established from the very foundation of the universe this conflict whose outcome has also been predicted: victory of Jesus Christ over Satan. Before turning to the Zodiac or the "gospel in the stars" we need to see the social context of development in the story of ancient Egypt.

1

THE STORY OF ANCIENT EGYPT

Much of what we know today about the Nile Valley civilization came to us only recently from archeologists. It all started with the "Rosetta Stone" found in Egypt by Napoleon's soldiers in 1799 which inspired Egyptologists to decipher the hieroglyphics. Then came the "Tell el Amarna tablets" which the late Sir Wallis Budge, the British archeologist and cuneiform expert, deciphered and considered to be of "very great importance".

The Tell el Amarna tablets were said to be "ancient and anguished cries for help from cities in Palestine and Syria to a Pharaoh about whom archeologists knew nothing but studies revealed him to be no less than "Amenhotep the Magnificent". Archeologists revealed a civilization which had been in existence over 3,000 years before Christ.

It was about 450 years BC when Herodotus, "the father of history" was said to have paid a long visit to ancient Egypt which had been the most famous and powerful country in the world. Payne writes: "At a time when the ancestors of Western man still lived as semi-savages in the dense forests of England and Europe, a great civilization existed along the banks of the Nile." A group of Egyptian priests took Herodotus to see the great pyramid of Giza—a "perfectly proportioned mountain of stone as high as a modern forty-story skyscraper" and a line of smaller pyramids stretched for more than sixty miles along the banks of the Nile (Payne 1964,43-44). This was not too far from the ancient capital city Memphis, where he stayed during his visit.

It was said that he stood "bareheaded and mute beneath Giza's towering sides", for nothing in all his travels had prepared him for such a sight. He learned from the priests that Giza had been the tomb of Pharaoh Cheops who had ruled Egypt more than 2,000 years earlier. The question is how did this civilization arise? This is what we will briefly investigate here.

The Nile River takes its source from what has later been named Lake Victoria in East Africa. It is about 4,000 miles long. We learn that prior to 25,000 years BC, what has become our present Sahara desert as a result of changes in the world climate, once supported life. As it dried up the only place left for human and animals was the Nile valley which measured about 750 miles long by thirty one miles wide toward its mouth or delta.

We understand that the river "teamed with fish, and the high reeds were alive with wild ducks, wild geese and water birds of all kinds". Great beasts entered the valley, which was the only source of water. First entered "giant bison, rhinos, elephants and smaller animals like wild pigs, dogs, gazelles and donkeys, hyenas and goats." After all these animals crept in the fear-filled men of that day" (ibid.,22-23).

According to archeologists, in a world populated by near-savages, the Nile Valley men learned to plant seeds and grow crops. They became farmers living in settled villages. They learned to tame animals such as goats, donkey and oxen. They discovered metal and used copper instead of stone tools and weapons. They learned to cook, sew, to spin and weave, to sculpt and paint; to add and subtract. Most exciting of all, they learned to read and write (ibid.,24).

Once a year the Nile flooded and left behind "Kemi" or silt, hence they called themselves the land of Kem or Kemit (Km't) as ancient Egypt was known. It was said that wherever the Nile flooded was Egypt, and whoever drank of or used its water was Egyptian.

Egyptian civilization and its beliefs could be traced as far back as 10,000-25,000 years BC, but its peak of development was reached about 3,200 BC when irrigation led to better agriculture which in turn led to specialization and exchange through barter trade. Political development emerged when villages were organized with gnomes or provinces and into kingdoms. At about 3,200BC there were three kingdoms. The delta region was ruled by the "Bee King" who ruled from a red house; a "Reed King" symbolized by a papyrus plant with a white crown ruled from a white house. This was the middle kingdom near the present location of Cairo.

Near the first cataract in Nubia was the Hawk King, whose standard copied the falcon that soared high in the sky. The Hawk King conquered the Reed and Bee Kings and united the kingdom into one at about 3,200 BC and his name was Menes, the first Pharaoh of ancient Egypt. To that time could be traced the roots of many concepts and beliefs that we hold today. These include beliefs about God, Satan, life after death, and such concepts that the Hebrews inherited from Egypt during their 430 years stay before the Exodus.

Some of these included the idea of divine kingship. They believed that their kings or Pharaohs, were semi-gods that were placed there to more easily communicate with the gods. They also believed that "they were the chosen people of the ancient world." All others were described as "vile" and "wretched" (ibid.,36). At the time that Joseph brought his family, shepherds by profession, to Egypt, the Egyptians regarded every shepherd as an "abomination". This was why they were settled in Goshen (Gen.46:34).

The social structure consisted of farmers, craftsmen and the nobility, including the priests who were just beneath Pharaoh who was considered divine—a god king. The nobility itself consisted of a privileged class made up of Pharaoh's relatives, and the descendants of pre-historic chieftains and kings.

Prof. Ben-Jochannan has summarized some of their achievements before Joseph and his father's household entered Sais (later called Egypt) as follows:

> "the indigenous Africans of Egypt had already become proficient in the sciences that allowed them to: a) embalm their dead; b)name

the bodies in the celestial universe; c) name their God and minor gods; d) develop agriculture; e) establish a solar calendar in 4,100 BC; f) develop a fertility control tampon recipe; g) build temples to the Gods—including the world-wonder, the Sphinx of Gezer (Giza); h)develop engineering; i)develop medicine, including internal surgery; j) develop pharmacology including many other disciplines such as the writing of short stories."
(Saakana Ed.1988,22-23).

This has been corroborated by Prof. George James, whose study of some basic questions concerning the Greeks overwhelmingly demonstrated that almost all that had been attributed to them actually originated from ancient Egypt. The questions were:

"Who were the Greek scholars? Where did they go to school? What did they learn in school? How old was the subject matter which they learned? Who were their teachers? How did what they learned fit with the contemporary Greek world view? How were they received home when they completed their education? How were they regarded by their teachers?" The result of this study was published in Stolen Legacy. Prof. Asa Hilliard asks some pertinent rhetorical questions which reflect on the general development of the ancient Egyptians. He asks: "Does it matter, contrary to contemporaneous teaching that:

1. 'Man know thyself' was not original with Socrates but was common among Egyptian teachers?

2. Plato's four cardinal virtues were copied from the Egyptian mysteries?

3. That grammar, rhetoric, logic, arithmetic, music, astronomy were Egyptian 'Liberal arts' copied by Greeks?

4. That whole Greek faculties and student bodies moved to Egypt to be taught by Egyptians and to learn from their libraries?

5. That Greek philosophers were not welcome at home?

6. That Greeks began going to Egypt for education around 525 BC?

7. That some of Plato's material comes from the 5,000 year old Egyptian Book of the Dead?

8. That the 4,000 year old Memphite Theology is the source of much of Greek thought?" (James:1978, Intro. To Reprint Ed.)

We have here the context of development which the environment of security over thousands of years provided for the nourishment of these complex achievements and religious systems such as the "Mysteries". This was the background from which emerged the savant astronomer-priests who laboriously mapped out the universe which has been inherited by all nations as the signs of the Zodiac which we will discuss in more detail in our next chapter.

2

GOD'S BLUEPRINT FOREVER SETTLED IN HEAVEN—THE ZODIAC

A "blueprint" means a detailed outline or plan. In this context, it means God's master plan for the world which is still unfolding. The savant or highly learned astronomer-priests of ancient Egypt after many years of careful observation of the heavenly bodies laboriously mapped out what is called the Zodiac. It is defined as: "an imaginary belt of the heavens centering on the ecliptic within which are the apparent paths of the sun, moon and principal planets" (Urdang 1973,1532).

A circular or elliptical diagram representing this belt contained pictures of beings and objects associated with the constellations and signs. The heavenly Zodiac was pictured as a great circular clock divided into twelve equal arcs or signs. These signs became the source of what is found all over the world. The twelve beings or signs are as follows: Virgo, Libra, Scorpio, Sagittarius, Capricorn, Aquarius, Pisces, Aries, Taurus, Gemini, Cancer and Leo.

In the Kamitic Genesis of Christianity Dr. Finch writes:

> "For uncounted generations lost in the dim mists of pre-historic antiquity, the Kamite astronomer-priests painstakingly mapped out all of the visible sky. They used typological nature symbols to create markers to help them chart the heavens. One product of that care-

ful labor is the Zodiac which the modern world inherited from the priests of Kemit" (Finch,1988:42).

Kemit, as pointed out, was the original name of ancient Egypt. These signs charted by these savant astronomer-priests of ancient Egypt became the source of what is found all over the world. It was they who mapped out what God had long established in the heavens–Christ—the seed of the woman to destroy the works of Satan (1John3:8b).

These have been established in the heavens not only to declare the glory of God but also to establish His supremacy over Satan and what He would attempt to do. As Dr. Kennedy points out: What God put in the stars is a glorious sky painting of Jesus Christ as the Lord of glory (Kennedy 1989,12). He states that nearly all nations had the same twelve signs, representing the same twelve things, placed in the same order but

> "Archeologists, historians, and antiquarians have searched the dustiest libraries, uncovered the oldest tablets, deciphered the most difficult hieroglyphics, and have failed to discover how it is that in so many nations all over the world the same signs exist" (ibid.,8).

It is curious that the place of origin of these signs should elude so many scholars. Could it be that prejudice has blinded them from admitting to ancient Egypt as the source since it is accepted as the cradle of civilization? Dr Kennedy states:

> "I know it will surprise you, but the sphinx actually unlocks the mystery of the Zodiac" (ibid.,21).

He notes that in the temple of Esneh in Egypt there is a great sky painting in the portico on the ceiling which shows the whole picture of the Zodiac with all its constellations. Between the figures of Virgo, the Virgin, and Leo, the Lion, there is carved the figure of the sphinx with the head of a woman and the body of a lion. The woman's face is looking at the Virgin and the lion's tail is pointing at Leo. He continues:

> "That same sphinx is found in the same place in a number of other great paintings of the Mazzaroth (or the constellations of the Zodiac), in other parts of the Near East, going back as much as 4,0000 years telling us the original place of beginning" (ibid.,21-22).

These have not only been passed on to the rest of the world and are found in that same order in all nations; many students of scriptures have also seen in them God's blueprint for the world. In Psalm 119:89 we read: "Forever, O Lord, Your word is settled in heaven". This statement confirms what God had established from the foundation of the universe. From this foundation, Jesus Christ, the Seed of the woman, had been established to destroy the works of the enemy, Satan. In another Psalm 19:1-3 we read:

> "The heavens declare the glory of God;
> And the firmament shows his handiwork.
> Day unto day utters speech,
> And night unto night reveals knowledge.
> There is no speech nor language
> Where their voice is not heard".

God had set down His blueprint and Psalm 2:3-4 states that the rulers of the world would try to overthrow the Lord's anointed but the Lord would have them in derision.

John's gospel (1:1) states: "In the beginning was the Word, and the Word was with God, and the Word was God". We are told that the Word became flesh and dwelt among us (and we beheld His glory as of the Father) full of grace and truth. This was Jesus about whom it was said, "Forever O Lord, your Word is settled in heaven" and also in Revelations referred to as "the Lamb slain from the foundation of the world" (Re.5:6b).

In Genesis (1:14) we read:

> "And God said, Let there be lights in the firmament of the heaven to divide the day from the night; and let them be for signs, and for seasons, and for days and years..."

We learn that this is not creation but the restoration of a perfect world that was destroyed as a result of Lucifer's rebellion.

Some titles pointing to the establishment of God's blueprint in the heavens include: "The Heavens Declare", (Banks, 1985); "The Hieroglyphics of the Heavens", (Carr-Harris, (1933); "God's voice in the Stars: Zodiac signs and Bible truth" (Flemming,1981); "Many infallible proofs", (Morris, 1974);"The Gospel in the Stars", (Seiss,1884). All these point to what has been established in the heavens since the foundation of the universe. They all speak about the same twelve signs from Virgo to Leo in that same order which is the order which we shall follow here basing our summary mostly on Dr. James Kennedy's latest book on the subject: "The Real Meaning of the Zodiac," (Kennedy,1989). We start with Virgo where the face of the sphinx with the head of the woman and the body of a lion is looking at the virgin.

Fig.1 following is an adaptation from "A PLANISPHERE OF THE HEAVENS" (Kennedy,1989) [originally taken from The gospel in the Stars (illustrated edition, Joseph Seiss,copyright,1972].

GOD'S BLUEPRINT FOREVER SETTLED IN HEAVEN—THE ZODIAC

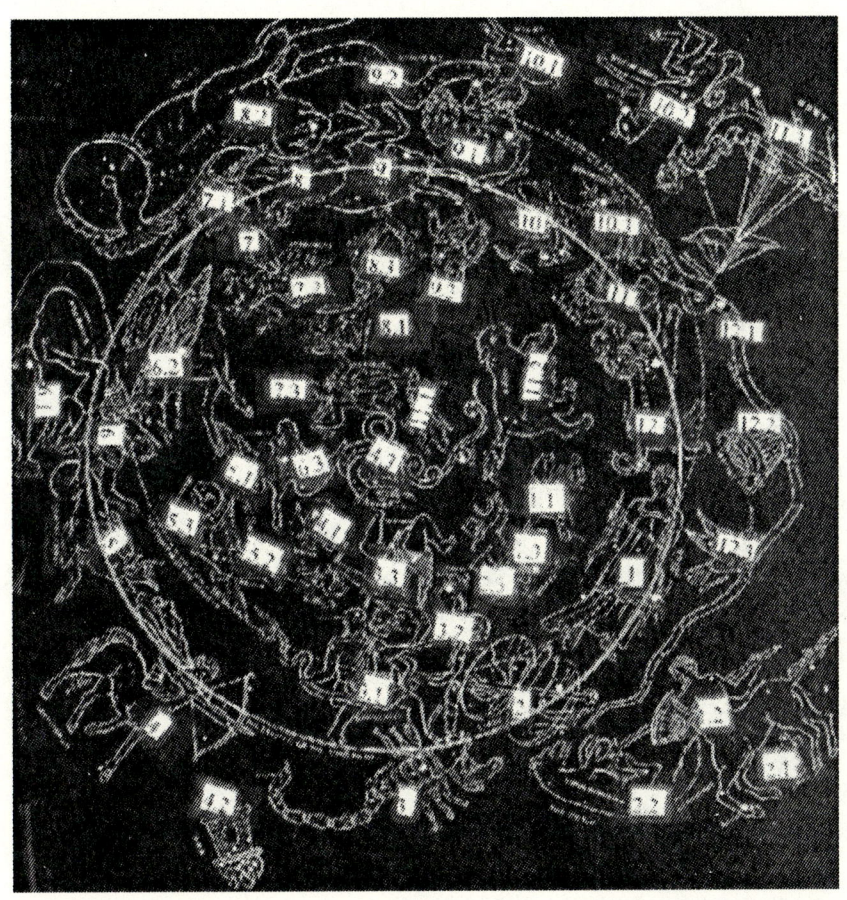

Fig.1

In order for us to more easily identify the typological signs, the "mansions" or "houses" have been identified numerically with their subdivisions as follows:

1. Virgo, the Virgin; 1.1 Coma, the Desired; 1.2 Centaurus, the Centaur; 1.3 Bootes, the Coming One.

The Virgin, the Desired, the Coming One all point to Jesus Christ while the Centaur and the Victim also point to His laying down His life.

"And I will put enmity between you and the woman, and between your seed and her Seed; He shall bruise your head, and you shall bruise His heal." (Ge.3.15).

Christ, the incarnate Son of God, fully divine and fully man would be the redeemer who would pay the full price of sin as shown by the sign Libra.

2. Libra, the Scales; 2.1 Crux, the Southern Cross; 2.2 Victima, the Victim; 2.3 Corona, the Crown.

The Scales or Balance, the Southern Cross, the Victim and the Crown are the required price to be paid on the cross for our redemption.

3. Scorpio, the Scorpion; 3.1 Orphiuchus, the Serpent holder; 3.2 Serpens, the Serpent; 3.3 Hercules, the Mighty One.

Scorpio and all its subdivisions record the mortal conflict between Christ and Satan. Isaiah writes:

> "He was wounded for our transgressions,
> He was bruised for our iniquities,"
> but the final triumph was in Sagittarius.

4. Sagittarius, the Archer; 4.1 Lyra, the Harp; 4.2 Ara, the Altar; 4.3 Draco, the Dragon. In all its sub-divisions, Sagittarius portrays Christ, the God-Man, as the victor over sin and Satan. John writes,

> "for this purpose the Son of God was manifested, that He might destroy the works of the devil" (1John3.8b).

5. Capricornus, the Goat; 5.1 Sagitta, the Arrow; 5.2 Aquila, the Eagle; 5.3 Dolphinus, the Dolphin. Capricornus, the Goat, (with Sagitta, the Arrow; Aquila, the Eagle and Dolphinus, the Dolphin)

GOD'S BLUEPRINT FOREVER SETTLED IN HEAVEN—THE ZODIAC

depicts life out of Christ's death for our sins which makes us spiritually alive as we find in John 12:24,

> "Most assuredly, I say to you, unless a grain of wheat falls into the ground and dies, it remains alone; but if it dies, it produces much grain."

6. Aquarius, the Water Bearer; 6.1 Piscis Australis, the Southern Fish; 6.2 Pegasus, the Winged Horse; 6.3 Cygnus, the Swan.

Aquarius, the Water Bearer, (with the Southern Fish, the Winged Horse and the Swan) depicts blessing out of victory. It speaks of the joy of God's Spirit poured out on His people. On the final and most important day of the feast, Jesus stood and called out:

> "If any one thirsts, let him come to me and drink...He who believes in Me...out of his heart will flow rivers of living water" (John7:37-38).

It was this Holy Spirit that the disciples were commanded to wait for in Jerusalem. He was the Power that started the church on the day of Pentecost.

7. Pisces, the Fishes; 7.1 the Band (connecting the two fishes under the paw of the Lamb); 7.2 Andromaeda, the chained Woman; 7.3 Cepheus, the Crowned King—the (Royal) Branch of the King–Christ enthroned.

Pisces, the sign of the fish, (with the Band connecting the two Fishes; Andromeda, the chained woman and Cepheus, the Crowned King) foretells God's deliverance out of bondage of people from all nations, from the slavery of sin, into the glorious light of His dear Son through the preaching of the gospel. He called His disciples to be fishers of men (Matt.4:19).

8. Aries, the Ram or Lamb; 8.1 Cassiopeia, the enthroned woman 8.2 Cetus, the Sea Monster; 8.3 Perseus, the Breaker.

Aries, the Ram or Lamb, (with Cassiopeia, the enthroned woman, Cetus, the Sea monster and Perseus, the Breaker) depicts glory out of humiliation. Christ laid down His life as the Lamb of God but took it back again through the help of the Holy Spirit and He became the ruler of all creation. In the revelation Jesus gave John, we hear the voice of

> "myriads of myriads and thousands of thousands, saying with a loud voice, 'Worthy is the Lamb that was slain to receive power and wealth and wisdom and strength and honor and glory and blessing'" (Re.5:12, MLB).

9. Taurus, the Bull; 9.1 Orion, the Glorious One; 9.2 Eridanus, the River; 9.3 Auriga, the Shepherd. Taurus, the Bull; Orion, the Glorious One; Eridanus, the River of the judge; and Auriga, the shepherd all point to His glorious coming in judgement, like a rampaging bull upon the sinful world. Long before Jesus came down from glory to fulfill God's blueprint the prophet Isaiah had a revelation from God of how it was all going to end.

> "Come here and listen, O nations of the earth;...For the Lord is enraged against the nations; His fury is against their armies. He will utterly destroy them and deliver them to slaughter. Their dead will be left out; the stench of their corpses shall rise, and the mountains shall melt in their blood. All the host of heaven shall dissolve, and the skies shall be rolled up like a scroll; all their host shall drop as leaves from the vine and as a fig falls from a fig tree." (Is.34:1-5 MLB).

10. Gemini, the Twins; 10.1 Lepus, the Enemy; 10.2 Canis Major, the Prince, (pictured as the Hawk, enemy of the Serpent); 10.3 Canis Minor, the Redeemer.

GOD'S BLUEPRINT FOREVER SETTLED IN HEAVEN—THE ZODIAC 21

Gemini the Twins, comprising Lepus, the Enemy; Canis Major and Minor, all depict Christ's union with His bride or fellowship with His people in eternal kingdom.

11. Cancer, the Crab consists of: 11.1 Ursa Minor, the Lesser Sheepfold; 11.2 Ursa Major, the Greater Sheepfold; and, 11.3 Argo, the Ship.

Cancer, the Crab; Ursa Minor and Major; Argo, the Ship all depict His possessions held secure with His kingdom filled with a multitude of people from every race, tribe, and nation. This too has been shown to John in Revelation.8:9:

> "And after this I looked and there was a vast host that no one could count out of all nations and tribes and peoples and tongues, standing before the throne and before the Lamb, clothed in white robes and with palm branches in their hands. And they shouted, "Salvation is due to our God who is seated on the throne, and to the Lamb".

What Jesus had revealed to John after His resurrection and is yet to be fulfilled at His second coming had actually been promised to Abraham in Ge.22:17 when he was obedient to God and almost sacrificed his only son Isaac. In this covenant God said,

> "I will greatly multiply your descendants so as to compare with the stars of heaven and the sand on the seashore for numbers."

12. Leo, the Lion comprises 12.1 Hydra, the Serpent; 12.2 Crater, the Cup;12.3 Corvus, the Raven. Leo, the Lion; Hydra, the Serpent; Crater, the Cup; and Corvus, the Raven, all point to the destruction of His enemies which prophetically assures us that Jesus Christ shall be victorious over sin, the world and Satan. This too was shown to John as the

"Lion out of the tribe of Judah, Offspring of David, has conquered so as to open the scroll and its seven seals" (Re.5:5).

In their original form and meaning, the signs of the Zodiac pointed to the conflict between Jesus and Satan and the enemy's ultimate defeat, which is yet to be completed at Jesus' Second Coming. In other words, the blueprint is still unfolding.

As is to be expected, corruption set in. The science of Astronomy became an Art of Astrology which distortion appears to have first emerged in Babylon, where the stars under which one was born was supposed to influence one's destiny. Coming a long way in time and space from the place of origin in ancient Egypt, we understand that the Babylonians were not even aware of the concept of "precession of the Equinoxes". This which factored in the tilting of the earth $23 \frac{1}{2}$ degrees on its axis meant that the signs moved some fifty seconds per year through the circle (Kennedy 1987,146). It is said that this resulted in the signs moving to positions of almost two months off, out of the "houses" where they belonged. This meant that predictions of the influence of the heavenly bodies based on the houses in which they were supposed to be, changed and were therefore false.

This is typical of Satan that initiated the war against God, as Lucifer before he was thrown out and became Satan. When Satan realized that God would use the Seed of the woman to destroy him, he became the force behind many schemes and influenced many different people to kill or corrupt the Seed of the woman. In a speech titled "The King still has one more move", Nancy Demoss detailed how Satan not only inspired Cain to kill his brother; he was the force behind Pharaoh's attempt to kill the sons of the Hebrews; he attempted to kill Jesus under King Herod. He not only attempted to defeat Jesus by having Him worship him Satan; he thought he had achieved victory over God when he instigated the Jews to have Barabas released and Jesus sent to the cross, until God proved to him that death was His weapon to overcome Satan.

It is therefore obvious that Satan would distort God's signs in the heavens that point to His glory, and His blueprint for the world to deceive many people in what we know today as horoscope. Astrology therefore became a popular means of misdirection to show how the heavenly bodies are supposed to influence one's life on earth.

God's people have been warned against worshipping the creatures rather than the Creator. In Romans 1:25 St. Paul writes that man

> "changed the truth of God into a lie, and worshipped and served the creature more than the Creator…"

Moses also warned the Hebrew people in their wilderness days, against worshipping the heavenly bodies.

> "Be thoroughly on guard therefore, with profoundest gravity, that you may not behave corruptly and fashion you an image the shape of any statue resembling either male or female, the likeness of any animal on earth, or of any bird that flies in the heavens…" (Deut.4:15-17).

Concerning astrology, God also warned His people through the prophet Isaiah:

> "You are exhausted due to your many plans; let the astrologers, the stargazers, and the monthly prognosticators stand up and save you from what shall come upon you. Take note! They shall all be like stubble, the fire shall consume them. They shall not be able to save themselves from the power of the flame…" (Is.47:13-14.MLB).

The apostle Paul writes in Romans1;20:

> "For since the creation of the world, His invisible attributes are clearly seen being understood by the things which are made, even His eternal power and Godhead, so that they are without excuse."

It is man's responsibility to study these signs and understand them. This was what the ancient Egyptians carefully mapped out showing the conflict between light and darkness, good and evil, God and Satan. Jesus, God the Son, is depicted in this master plan as having the final victory over Satan.

The fulfillment of the blueprint was God's initiative just as was the detailed outline itself. He called Abraham from Babylon where the corruption most likely originated. He established the Jewish people through bondage in Egypt. He called Moses to bring them out, and after the prophets, priests and kings, God sent Jesus as the final disclosure of Himself.

Over the millennia, the ancient Egyptians have come to learn much about God, Satan and Man. Their concepts about these have been practically the same ideas we hold today and our next chapter will discuss them in some detail.

3

THE ANCIENT EGYPTIANS' CONCEPT OF GOD AND OF SATAN

From the discussion of the Zodiac, it would seem obvious that the ancient Egyptians had a revelation from God because they received the blueprint of God's original purposes for the world. These they carefully mapped out from their careful observation of the heavens. From this they developed their concept of God Almighty, which appears to be the same inherited by Christianity today.

There has been little change from the ancient Egyptian's conception of God Almighty from what we know about Him today. It would seem that the only change has been God's later revelation of Himself through the Son, Jesus Christ. There is also the Power of the Holy Spirit in His own life and His present work in the Church. But their understanding of God Almighty as Creator of all things has been the basic foundation and the root upon which our understanding of God is based.

The late Prof. Wallis Budge, Keeper of the Egyptian and Assyrian Antiquities in the British Museum, takes issue with writers who have focused on the many gods worshipped by the ancient Egyptians and not on their understanding of who the Almighty was as mapped out in the sky. He writes:

> "A study of ancient Egyptian religious texts will convince the reader that the Egyptians believed in One God, who was self-exis-

tent, immortal, invisible, eternal, omniscient, almighty, and inscrutable; the maker of the heavens, earth, and underworld; the creator of the sky and the sea, men and women, animals and birds, fish and creeping things, trees and plants, and the incorporeal beings who were the messengers that fulfilled his wish and word" (Budge 1978,17).

He also points out that however far back we follow his literature,

"we never seem to approach a time when he was without this remarkable belief" (ibid.,18).

For those in the Evolutionist camp, it is instructive to note what God, the Almighty, said:

"I evolved the evolving of the evolutions. I developed Myself from the primeval matter which I made…Nothing existed on this earth then, and I made all things…I performed all evolutions there by means of that divine soul which I fashioned there, and which had remained inoperative in the watery abyss. I emitted from Myself the gods Shu and Tefnu, and from being One I became three…" (Ibid.,42).

We understand that all these happened in the dateless past when God's creation became "inoperative in the watery abyss" which is an indication of Lucifer's rebellion and destruction when God commanded the sun not to rise; sealed off the stars; and treaded on the waves of the sea or as the Spirit of God hovered over the face of the waters (Job 9:7-8; Gen.1:2). Here then is an indication of the source of what we find in Job, the oldest book in the Bible, as well as what we find in the dateless past according to Gen.1:1. This also means that long before Evolutionists came on the scene, the Word of God Himself had indicated how it all began and it could not have been without Him. We are also introduced to the Trinity–God the Father, God the Son, and God the Holy Spirit.

Alongside the belief in the Almighty God there also developed polytheistic ideas and beliefs, which the ancient Egyptian cultivated at different periods in history. The "gods" are said to be only "forms, manifestations, and phases of Ra, the Sun-god, who was himself the type and symbol of God…" (Ibid.35). As quoted by Budge, one Dr. Brugsch collected a number of epithets which were applied to the gods from texts of all periods. From these one could see that the ideas and beliefs of the ancient Egyptians concerning God "were almost identical with those of the Hebrews and Mohammedans at a later period."

Some of these ideas were as follows:

> "God is One and alone, and none other existeth with Him; God is the One, the One who made all things…God is a Spirit, a hidden spirit, the spirit of spirits, the great spirit of the Egyptians, the divine spirit…He is truth, the Eternal One…He is not only truth, and liveth by truth; God is life and through Him only man liveth…He gives life to man and He breathed the breath of life into his nostrils…He is both father of fathers and mother of mothers…God Himself is existence, and He liveth in all things…God hath created the universe and all things that therein is…God is the father of the gods, and the father of the father of all deities. He is the great Master, the primeval Potter who turneth men and gods out of His hands, and He formed men and gods upon a potter's table…God is merciful unto those who reverence Him, and he heareth him that calleth upon Him. He protecteth the weak against the strong, and He heareth the cry of him that is bound in fetters…he judgeth between the mighty and the weak. God knoweth him that knoweth Him, He rewardeth Him that serveth Him, and He protecteth him that followeth Him" (Budge:37-40 as quoted from Brugsch).

It is necessary to quote these sources at length to establish the fact that our concept of God: His nature and character, His creation and relationship to other gods had long been known and established in ancient Egypt most likely by the same savant astronomer-priests that laboriously mapped out the Zodiac.

Compare the concept of God developed then and our ideas of God today.

Very little has changed except the dimensions in terms of the love of God added by Jesus Christ, as was Pharaoh Akhnaton's conception of God earlier.

In Prayers that Avail Much put out by Word Ministries (1994) we read:

> I worship and adore You, El-Elyon, the Most High God Who is the First Cause of everything, the Possessor of the Heavens and earth. You are the Everlasting-God, the Great-God, the Living-God, the Merciful God. You are Truth, Justice, Righteousness, and Perfection. You are El-Elyon–the Highest Sovereign of the heavens and earth. Halloweth be They name!
>
> It continues:
>
> Father, You have exalted above all else Your name and Your Word, and You have magnified Your Word above all Your name! The Word was made flesh, and dwelt among us, and His name is JESUS! Halloweth be Thy name!

Along with this lofty concept of God, the "One One," and "the Ancient of Days", developed a high moral code as found in the "Negative Confessions" better translated "The Declaration of Innocence before the Gods of the Tribunal". The declaration of innocence took place before forty-two gods who represented the gnomes or regions of ancient Egypt. The deceased declared to the tribunal of forty-two gods that he had not committed a series of specific sins, which in Egyptian eyes apparently covered every conceivable kind of wrongdoing. The heart was weighed in the scales of the balance against the "feather of righteousness," which would mean that it was the quality of the heart that was being measured and not the weight.

God was the One, Self-begotten, and Self-existent One whom the Egyptians worshipped and was associated with the Sun—Ra. He was the Power of Powers.

> "Behold, thou art the everlasting creator, and thou art adored [as such when] thou settest in the heavens...Thou makest the generations of man to flourish through the Nile flood, and thou cause gladness to exist in all lands, and in all cities, and in all temples...O thou mighty one of victories, thou Power of Powers, who dost make strong thy throne against evil fiends—thou who art glorious in Majesty..." (Budge 1978,54).

But it is also important not to create the impression that the ancient Egyptians focused only on one God. Not even the Hebrew people focused on the one God that delivered them out of Egyptian bondage. The Egyptians paid homage to a number of gods but it was said that the educated classes at all times never placed the gods on the same high level as God.

In a chapter on "Gods" of the Egyptians, Sir Wallis Budge tells us that every family of any wealth and position had its own god. The wealthy family selected someone to attend to its god. The upkeep of the god may be contributed to by the poor. The overthrow of the family included the overthrow of the god. The god of the village might be led into captivity along with people of the village, but the victory of his followers in a raid or fight caused his honors to be enhanced.

There were also gods of great cities and provinces. Sometimes the attributes of two gods may be fused or united to form one. Sometimes gods were imported from remote villages and towns and even from foreign countries. Occasionally a community or town would repudiate its god or gods, and adopt a brand new set from a neighboring district (Budge 1978,109-110).

Besides family and village gods, there were national gods and gods of rivers and mountains, and gods of earth and sky, all of which taken together made a formidable number of "divine" beings whose goodwill had to be secured, and whose ill will must be appeased. Besides these, a number of animals regarded as being sacred to the gods were also considered to be "divine" and fear as well as love made the Egyptians add to their numerous classes of gods (ibid.,110).

This was the cultural background from which God removed the Hebrew people and we can see more clearly God's disappointment expressed through Jeremiah in the question:

> "What injustice did your fathers find in Me, that they abandoned Me, habitually followed after futility, and became useless?...My people have committed two evils: they have forsaken Me the Fountain of living waters, and they have hewn out for themselves cisterns, broken cisterns, which cannot hold water" (Jer.2:5, 13MLB).

Even when God freed them from Egyptian bondage their cultural background stayed with them and that included changing gods for any reason, including the Almighty God Himself.

Osiris, the God of the resurrection.

According to Budge, the Egyptians of every period believed that Osiris was of divine origin, that he suffered death and mutilation at the hands of the powers of evil; that after a great struggle with these powers, he rose again, and that he became henceforth the king of the underworld and judge of the dead, and that because he had conquered death, the righteous also might conquer death (ibid.,61).

They raised Osiris to such an exalted position in heaven that he became the equal (and in certain cases the superior of Ra) the Sun god and ascribed unto him the attributes which belong unto God.

> "He represented to men the idea of a man who was both god and man, and he typified to the Egyptians of all ages the being who by reason of his sufferings and death as a man could sympathize with them in their own sickness and death" (ibid.,81).

They believed that they, like him, would rise again and inherit life everlasting. He who was the son of Ra was said to have become the equal of his father, and he took his place side by side with him in heaven. He was not only god and judge of the dead but also creator of the world and of all things in it (ibid.,83). Hebrews (1:1-14) tells us that Jesus was exalted above all Angels.

> "But to the Son He says:
> 'Your throne, O God, is forever and ever;
> A scepter of righteousness is the scepter of Your Kingdom'
> (Heb.1:8).

He was called God by God the Father and we see how God has highly exalted and given Him a name which is above every name (Ph.2:9). The reasons for this exaltation will be explained later but Osiris became the prototype that Jesus came to fulfill. From being a god of the dead, Osiris became a dead god after Christ came to fulfill and not to destroy. To the Christians of Egypt, at least, his place was filled by Christ, according to Budge.

The ancient Egyptian's lived with eternity in view. Life was lived in the knowledge that it was not eternal, unlike life after death. This understanding led to the development of a moral code, which molded their behavior. After death was the judgement already referred to above as the "Declaration of Innocence" or the "Negative Confessions".

A few of these confessions were:

> "I have not robbed...stolen...told lies...committed perjury; committed homosexuality; reviled or blasphemed God."...

In fact Prof. Ben-Jochannan points out that the Ten Commandments were only ten of more than one hundred and forty seven "laws the indigenous Africans had written before the first Haribu (Jew), Abraham, entered Sais (Egypt)" (Saakana,Ed.,25). He states that: "the co-option of the sacred scriptures by various religious groups was common among the ancients" (ibid.).

By "co-option" here is meant that they had free access to and integrated in their knowledge and understanding previous knowledge and information which they used freely. He compares the teachings of

Amen-em-ope, Pharaoh of Egypt (1405-1370 BC) with the teachings of King Solomon of Israel (1976-936 BC) in Proverbs. He claimed that Solomon "too often copied Amen-em-ope in too many instances word for word" (Ibid.,25). Two such examples of Amen-em-ope's are:

> Beware of robbing the poor, and of oppressing the afflicted; or A scribe who is skillful in his business findeth himself worthy to be a courtier.

Both teachings are found in Solomon's proverbs as follows:

> Rob not the poor because he is poor: neither oppress the afflicted in the gate:... (Prov.22:22); or
> Seest thou a man diligent in his business? He shall stand before kings; he shall not stand before mean men (Prov.22:29).

Moses who was trained in the wisdom of the Egyptians and groomed to become the next Pharaoh had access to all the information concerning the wisdom of the Egyptians, in addition to what God revealed to him personally. If it was not illegal to use sources of knowledge from previous generations without giving credit to the original authors, it is not unlikely that Moses would do the same with reference to all the Egyptian wisdom found in the Book of the Dead or originating from oral tradition. But this does not invalidate the fact that God called him and spoke as well as revealed certain things to him personally. It is also necessary to point out that the Holy Spirit is the original Author of the Bible and that what others wrote at different time periods in history only reported what the Holy Spirit had previously revealed to others. Since it is the same source, it did not invalidate God's Word.

The Ancient Egyptian's concept of Satan

According to Prof. Finch: "The Great Adversary in the Kamitic schema is Set who as "Set-an" gives his name to the Judeo-Christian

Satan" (Finch, in Saakana, Ed.,53). Set's color was red, and was sometimes personified as a goat in ancient Egypt. Satan was represented in the Zodiac first as **Scorpio** that stings the mighty man Orphiucus in the heel. We have here a picture of this great Scorpion and a blueprint of his battle with Christ" (Kennedy 1989,41). We see him also represented as a **serpent** that wriggles and struggles in the firm grip of Orphiucus and reaching up to take the crown away from God, just as we are told in the Old Testament that Lucifer attempted to do and was cast out of heaven by God (Is.14:12). Satan is then represented as **Cetus**, the sea monster and his attempt to destroy Pisces, the fishes, representing the people of God. Cetus is, however, tied by a band that is held under the foot of Aries, the Lamb. Here again we see Christ's control over the work of Satan.

Satan is again represented as a **lion** that is destroyed by Orion (Christ) Who holds his dead carcass. We then find Satan represented by the head of the gorgon **Medusa** with serpents for his hair. He is slain by Perseus, another picture of Christ. Finally, Satan is represented by **Hydra**, the Great Serpent who covers so much of the sky. But he is finally destroyed by the lion (of the tribe of Judah) Jesus Christ; by the outpouring of the cup of wrath, and by the devouring fowls of the air depicted in Corvus, the Raven.

In all these representations of Satan and his conflict with Christ, the latter always came out victorious.

The concepts of God and of Satan discussed above are practically the same ideas seen in both the Old and the New Testaments. The blueprint has been clearly established as the foundation and bedrock on which was built the creation story in Genesis. It provided the same foundation for the "proto evangelium" the first preaching of the gospel concerning the serpent and the seed of the woman (Kennedy 1989,11). The rest of the Old and New Testaments confirm the same. Later revelations directly from God came through the prophets, kings and priests, with the ultimate disclosure of God the Father coming through the Son when He came "to fulfill and not to destroy" (Matt.5:17b). He sent the Holy Spirit to continue the work of salvation through repentance and forgiveness of sins.

Such concepts as God and Satan might strike some as ideas and possibly myths. Despite many satanic activities and the satanic spirit behind many things that happen today, few people even believe in the existence of Satan because one cannot see it as a spirit. Similarly, the idea of God as Spirit confounds many individuals who will believe only what they can experience with their five senses.

Unlike Satan that can only occupy human bodies or the bodies of animals, God the Father showed Himself in the Son, Jesus Christ, who actually came to show man the way. Long before this, man made sincere efforts to reach God. It was naturally the ancient Egyptians who initiated this effort and religions that followed that pattern exercised and focused on "works" as the means of reaching God.

The ancient Egyptians had developed a very complex religious system called the "Mysteries", according to Prof. George James in **Stolen Legacy** (1978). The Mysteries, as the first system of salvation, "was man's first attempt to reach God." It regarded the human body as a prison house of the soul which could be liberated through the discipline of the Arts and Sciences and "advanced from the level of a mortal to that of a God" (James 1978,1). Consequently practically all religions followed this practice. Most religions, including Judaism, sought to use works or man's effort to do something as a means to appease, please or reach God. Only in Christianity do we see God as the initiator:

> "For God so loved the world that He gave his only begotten Son, that whosoever believeth in Him should not perish, but have everlasting life" (John 3:16).

Whereas man was the center and initiator of the effort to reach God in all other religions, only in Christianity does the initiative come from God. He is the center and the initiator of the act of salvation through the Lord Jesus Christ as He had long established it in the heavens through the blueprint.

Until the coming of Jesus, it was obvious that God had not yet fully disclosed Himself. Anything that was established was not based on God's total revelation of Himself through the Son and the need to deal with the problem of sin. Only Jesus dealt with that problem when He became sin for us. But even after the revelation of God through Jesus Christ, the Jewish people still clung to their idea of good "works". In Romans 10:2-3 Paul acknowledges that the Jewish people have a zeal for God.

> "I know what enthusiasm they have for the honor of God, but it is misdirected zeal. For they don't understand that Christ has died to make them right with God. Instead they are trying to make themselves good enough to gain God's favor by keeping the Jewish laws and customs, but that is not God's way of salvation" (LB).
> Jesus said: "I am the Way, the Truth and the Life. No one comes to the Father except through Me" (John 14:6).

In our next chapter, we will consider the concept of man and his interactions with God and Satan.

4

THE ANCIENT EGYPTIANS' CONCEPT OF MAN

The ancient Egyptians believed that, like all other things found in the universe, man was created by God Almighty. They believed that only God had the power to cause men "to be born again" or be born into a new life beyond the grave which is everlasting life. These and many truths have been recorded in the Book of the Dead.

Pre-dynastic man believed in a material resurrection, with the dead living again in identical bodies, hence the emphasis on mummification. Bodily resurrection was later replaced by the belief that the material part of man rests on the earth whilst the immaterial part has its abode in heaven. This was exemplified in such statements addressed to the dead as:

> "Ra receive thee, soul in heaven, body in earth", or "Thine essence is in heaven, thy body is in the earth" (Book of the Dead, Intro.Iv1).

Man was therefore conceived as not just physical but mostly spiritual. Over the centuries nine aspects of man had been identified, some of which overlapped, but these formed the basis of the three aspects of man identified by Christians as body, soul and spirit. The ancient Egyptians identified man as having been created with the following nine components:

1. "Khat" or the physical body which was liable to decay.

2. The "ka" (or kla as known in Dangbe, the writer's local African language) is the "double" or the abstract individuality or personality which possessed the form and attributes of the man to whom it belongs. They believed that it could get out of the body in the tomb and wander about at will if not properly supplied with food.

3. The "ba" or the heart-soul was connected with the "ka". This was made to live with Ra or Osiris in heaven.

4. The "ab" or heart was closely associated with the soul and was held to be the "source both of the animal life and of good and evil in man. The preservation of the heart of a man was held to be of the greatest importance, and in the judgement, it is the one member of the body singled out for special examination." It is regarded as having been the center of the spiritual and the thinking life and as the organ through which the manifestations of virtue and vice revealed themselves. It typified everything that "conscience" typifies to us.

The other five aspects will be briefly mentioned. They include the "khaibit" or shadow; "khu" or spiritual soul; "sekhem" or the incorporeal personification of the vital force of man; the "ren" or name and finally, the "sahu" or the spiritual body which formed the habitation of the soul (Budge: Book of the Dead, Iix-lxvii).

From all this derived the Christian concept that man is a spirit that has a soul and lives in a body. Such statements by Jesus of the need to "be born again" or the importance given to the "heart" as the source of good and evil derived from this understanding. Proverbs 4:23 states:

> "Keep your heart with all diligence, For out of it springs the issues of life." In Matthew 15:19

Jesus explained to his disciples:

"For out of the heart proceed evil thoughts, murders, adulteries, fornication, thefts, false witness, blasphemies".

These are the things that defile a person, according to Jesus. From this and many other concepts that Jesus used, we could see that he embraced concepts that had their origin in ancient Egypt, just as all the prophets starting with Moses.

The significance for us today of what ancient Egyptians thought about God, Man and Satan.

The ancient Egyptians had the longest experience at the game of life. As such the lessons they learned should be of value to us if we are also to benefit from their experiences. Much of what they learned about God, Satan and Man, life after death, the judgment, and what moral laws needed to be followed to maintain a good social order have been recorded in "The book of the Dead", their "Mysteries" and other documents of Arts and Sciences. Many of these have later been attributed to the Greeks, according to Prof. George James in "Stolen Legacy" (1978). These concepts also form the foundation of the Bible. To the extent that we disregard what is in the Bible, to that extent we cut ourselves off from the wisdom of the ages and the benefits we can derive from their experiences.

From them we learn that man was created by God, and that he was not just an accident of creation. Man was therefore accountable to God. He is not only flesh that lives and dies; he is more of a spirit that has a soul or consciousness which includes his mind and will. Both spirit and soul live in a body. After the body dies, the spirit is released for judgement to live either in heaven or in hell.

We learn from them also that there is conscience built into man. Just the same way that man responds to the physical universe and its laws, so also does he respond to the moral laws of the universe. God created both. The law of sin and death operates side by side with the law of life in Christ Jesus, just as there is the law of gravity. Man ignores God's moral laws at his own peril. These concepts have also been recorded in the Bible. Modern man can deny the fact of creation but that does not change the truth of moral and physical laws. Ignorance is no excuse either.

The law of the Spirit of Life in Christ Jesus operates by faith in Him; its "currency" is faith in the Word of God that secures from Him what one needs. On the other hand, money is the currency that the god of this world uses to rule. He uses it as a bait to hook many into schemes that may give them fame, fortune, power and other forms of recognition by the world. It however, leaves one empty and dissatisfied because a God-shaped vacuum is created in the heart and this can only be filled by God.

While one is focused on the things of the world, one cannot serve God. Jesus said: "You cannot serve God and Mammon" (Matt.6:24b). He also said "It is the Spirit who gives life; the flesh profits nothing." (John 6:63a). The exclusion of God from one's knowledge leads to serious consequences. In Romans 1:28-32 Paul lists some of these:

> "And even as they did not like to retain God in their knowledge, God gave them over to a debased mind, to do those things that are not fitting; being filled with all unrighteousness, sexual immorality, wickedness, covetousness, maliciousness; full of envy, murder, strife, deceit, evil-mindedness…"

These are but a few of the list of things a debased mind is subject to.

When man does not recognize the reality of God, he also fails to recognize the reality of Satan and that Satan is a destroyer, and that in his camp there is no love, joy or peace regardless of how much of these world's goods one possesses.

Another consequence is that man can never rise to fulfill his potential God has for him. He is cut off from the knowledge and wisdom of God. That ideal stature is found only in Jesus Christ. Man is supposed to grow "to a perfect man, to the measure of the stature of the fullness of Christ" (Ephesians 4:13b). Aside from all these, there are areas of knowledge that are totally out of the domain of those outside of Christ. The Power of the Living God is totally out; so are healing miracles; Word of knowledge and of Wisdom. These do not include wisdom from God in the Proverbs many of which can be traced to Amen-em-ope, Pharaoh of ancient Egypt (1405-1370BC).

Any educational system that seeks to exclude God from its knowledge has seriously compromised the potential its students can reach. It is the greatest disservice and deprivation students can experience. American Public School system is seriously at fault here because the foundation of education and of knowledge has been corroded. We will expound on this in our final chapter on conclusions and implications. Our next chapter will briefly discuss the dynamic interaction between God, Satan and Man.

5

THE DYNAMIC RELATIONSHIP BETWEEN GOD, SATAN AND MAN.

Once to every **man** and nation
Comes the moment to **decide**
In the **strife** of **truth** with **falsehood**
For the **good** or **evil** side.

This short verse from an old hymn shows that there is a dynamic relationship that exists in life in the struggle between truth and falsehood; between the good and evil side. How was this conflict initiated? We are told that it started with Satan against God before man came on the scene. This conflict led to Satan being thrown out of heaven. This idea was recorded in the Bible by the prophet Isaiah (14:12)

"How you are fallen from heaven,
O Lucifer, son of the morning!
How you are cut down to the ground,
You who weakened the nations!"

The original of this is found in the Book of the Dead.

"Thine enemy the Serpent hath been given over to the fire, the Serpent-fiend Sebau hath fallen down headlong; his arms have been bound in chains, and thou hast hacked off his legs; and the sons of impotent revolt shall never more rise up against thee" (Budge 1951,48).

Man finds himself involved in this conflict by virtue of being born into this world. There are two camps and there is no middle ground. Participation is not by choice; it is simply what life is made of. Man as a free-will agent has to make that choice between good and evil, Christ and Satan. According to Genesis, our original parents made the wrong choice by listening to Satan who suggested to them that God did not have their best interest at heart and that they could do better for themselves by being disobedient to God. They went with the devil and this bent toward evil continues with man today. He finds it easier to choose the wrong and finds evil more attractive. But God Who anticipated this fall provided the remedy through the Seed of the woman, Jesus Christ, Who has been shown in the Zodiac as the One come to overcome Satan and to destroy the works of darkness. He said:

> "The thief does not come except to steal, and to kill, and to destroy. I have come that they may have life and that they may have it more abundantly" (John10:10).

Before this, we find Moses in the Old Testament admonishing the Israelites in Deuteronomy 30:19;

> "I call heaven and earth as witnesses today against you, that I have set before you life and death, blessing and cursing; therefore choose life, that you and your descendants may live;..."

St. Paul writes:

> "For we do not wrestle against flesh and blood, but against principalities, against powers, against the rulers of the darkness of this age, against spiritual hosts of wickedness in the heavenly places" (Eph.6:12).

This warfare or conflict has been between good and evil, light and darkness, right and wrong, truth and falsehood, virtue and vice, God and Satan. This has been established from the beginning and when man came on the scene he had no choice but to interact and dynamically participate. We are assured of victory when on the side of Jesus, who said: "I am the Way, the Truth and the Life" (John 14:6). He also points out that there are only two ways: the broad and narrow way, and that only the narrow way leads to salvation: "For there is One God, and one Mediator between God and men, The Man Christ Jesus" (Timothy 2:5).

In this dynamic interaction between Man, Satan and God we find that two laws have been established: The law of sin and death and the law of the Spirit of Life in Christ Jesus (Rom.8:2). These laws rule in the two kingdoms that had been established—that of God and of Satan. Satan's leads to death and destruction. It is described as walking in the flesh. Walking in the Spirit, however, leads to life. "The law of the Spirit of life in Christ Jesus has made me free from the law of sin and death". Christ stands for one and Satan for the other. Faith in Jesus Christ connects one to life and liberty in Him.

When Jesus started His ministry He read from Isaiah (61:1-2) as recorded by Luke (4:18):

> "The Spirit of the Lord is upon Me,
> Because He has anointed Me to preach the gospel to the poor,
> He has sent Me to heal the broken hearted,
> To preach deliverance to the captives
> And recovery of sight to the blind,
> To set at liberty those who are oppressed,
> To preach the acceptable year of the Lord."

Jesus was anointed to correct the enemy's destructive work. Satan had man in the grip of sin and its consequences: poverty, being broken hearted; being in captivity or slavery to sin; spiritual blindness, and the spirit of oppression have all been the work of Satan. Jesus came for the purpose of destroying the work of Satan as we are told in 1 John (3:8b).

> "For this purpose Christ was manifested
> That He might destroy the works of darkness".

How valid are these claims? Is He indeed the Way, the Truth and the Life? What about other religious leaders and their claims? It is interesting to note that no other religious leader claimed to be **the only way**. They all claimed to be one of the ways to God. In all of them man was the center or initiator. Man attempted to do something to please God. But as long as the problem of sin has not been solved, man is still in Satan's camp. Only the blood of Jesus Christ paid the full price, which was confirmed by His resurrection from the dead. He also said He would ask the Father to send the Holy Spirit back to earth to be the Teacher, Guide and Comforter of His people (John16:13-15). The Holy Spirit would not speak on His own authority but whatever He hears He would speak.

> "He will glorify Me, for He will take of what is Mine and declare it to you"(ibid.).

The Holy Spirit came and He has been at work from the establishment of the Church since the time of Pentecost. It is only Jesus whose tomb is empty and who claims to be alive and well. Rev.18 states:

> "I am He who lives, and was dead, and behold,
> I am alive forever more.."

The Holy Spirit brings the presence of Jesus when His people are led in praise and worship, and wonderful things happen in the name of Jesus. These include miracle healing of numerous diseases and conditions that medical doctors have given up on. They include "word of knowledge" describing the disease or something that happened years ago. People not even present at the place of worship also receive healing.

To my knowledge, I know of no other "ways" that claim to bring their worshippers to the presence of God and for miracles to happen. It is true that Satan could counterfeit some miracles but the god of this world often takes back more from his people than he can give. Even when Satan entices people with wealth, fame, power and other things that are attractive to men, they realize the emptiness of it all. Only Christ satisfies.

6

"I AM NOT COME TO DESTROY, BUT TO FULFIL" (Mt. 5:17b)

The Living Bible puts it this way:

> "Do not misunderstand why I have come—it isn't to cancel the laws of Moses and the warnings of the prophets. No, I came to fulfill them and to make them all come true. With all the earnestness I have I say: Every law in the Book will continue until its purpose is achieved" (Mt. 5:17-18 LB).

Those listening to Jesus Christ were encouraged to look to the Old Testament as their guide but not to the examples of the leaders. He came to fulfill the symbols of the law. He came to fill up the defects of it, and to complete and perfect it. Christ made an improvement of the law and the prophets by His additions and explications (Church Ed.,1992). They were to exceed the righteousness of the scribes and Pharisees.

What were some of the laws of Moses? How did he come by them? How did Jesus extend these laws so as to "fulfill" them?

Under the laws of Moses, some of the rules said: "If you kill, you must die", but Jesus extended it to say that if you are only angry even in your own home, you are in danger of judgement. Another rule said, "You shall not commit adultery". But Jesus said: "Anyone who even looks at a woman with lust in his eye has already committed adultery with her in his heart". Here we find the importance of the "heart-soul" as the source of all motivation; the source or fountain of good and evil. It is this source that should be guarded with all diligence, for out of it "spring the issues of life" (Prov.4:23).

Another law of Moses said "if anyone wants to be rid of his wife, he can divorce her merely by giving her a letter of dismissal". Here too the only ground that Jesus would accept divorce is fornication or adultery (Mt5:21-32). The Sermon on the Mount was devoted to extending and explicating the meaning of the laws. These truly fulfilled the laws and therefore exceeded the righteousness of the scribes and Pharisees who saw themselves justified when they fulfilled the outward requirements of the law. Jesus went deeper to the motives behind every action.

We now turn to the question: How did Moses come by these laws? We read that Moses was adopted by the daughter of Pharaoh who brought him up to be her own son.

> "So Moses was educated in all the science and learning of the Egyptians and had ability in speech and in deeds" (Acts 7:22MLB).

He was actually being raised to become the next Pharaoh, and so he was exposed to all the knowledge and wisdom of the ages. He was highly educated and prepared for his position until God called and separated him from the Egyptian background through the accident of killing Pharaoh's officer, his brother African of non-Jewish religion, when he interceded for his Hebrew brother. He became a shepherd for forty years until he died to self before God could use him for His work. This means that God could not use him until the self, which is sin, is totally submitted to God. It was at this point that God's power flowed through him. He became the fuse that conducted the Power of God.

At this point, Moses did not just depend on the worldly wisdom and education he received; he was prepared to be completely dependent on God and His directions. The Ten commandments he received from Mount Sinai were said to have been carved in stone tablets with the finger of God. Even if these came from a reservoir of laws, as has been argued elsewhere, they were still chosen by God as the basic minimum for His people at the time. They also happen to be the foundation of Western law still used to guide modern civilization. Because Moses was fully dead to self and completely dependent on God to pull them out of bondage in Egypt, take them across the Red Sea and provide miraculously for them, there is no reason not to believe that God gave Him those commandments as reported in the Bible.

What about the ideas and concepts that existed thousands of years before Jesus came on the scene, including His own image as represented in the Zodiac by the ancient savant astronomer-priests? Prophecies about the birth of Jesus were given about 750 years before His birth. In Isaiah (9:6) we read:

> "For unto us a child is born, Unto us a son is given;
> And the government will be upon his shoulder.
> And his name will be called Wonderful, Counselor, Mighty
> God, Everlasting Father, Prince of Peace."

This prophecy was much closer to the time of His appearance from glory than the revelations given to those who mapped out the Zodiac thousands of years earlier. But since it is from the same source, the Holy Spirit, it is to be expected that there would be no inconsistency. Therefore as Jesus fulfilled the relatively more recent prophecies, He also automatically fulfilled much earlier revelations about Him and what He was coming to do. Similarly, as He fulfilled the laws and the prophets, He was fulfilling laws that God had given His people thousands of years before the birth of Moses himself.

The Bible says that God is no "respecter of persons" (Acts10:34); this means that God is not partial. Peter came to this realization when he said:

> "I see very clearly that the Jews are not God's only favorites! In every nation he has those who worship Him and do good deeds and are acceptable to him (Acts10:34-35,LB).

We can safely say that He revealed Himself to the ancient Egyptians the same way He revealed himself to the Jewish people. For it was the same God Almighty these Africans of the Nile Valley worshipped. The native Africans knew Him by the name "Ra", the sun being His symbol. The native Africans of Hebrew background referred to Him as "Yahweh". We are told how Joseph was hastily taken out of prison to interpret a dream to Pharaoh. "Then Joseph said to Pharaoh, the (two) dreams are one; God has shown Pharaoh what He is about to do." Joseph went on to explain to Pharaoh what God was showing him through the dream of the seven good cows and the seven good ears of grain and their opposites. This would mean that God had been communicating with people from time immemorial but especially with those who had dedicated their lives to Him as the astronomer-priests to whom God revealed the blueprint of His creation.

According to archeologists, as reported by Payne, long before the ancient world was ready or able to accept such a concept, and long before the time of Joseph and of the Hebrews, Akhnaton had reached the conclusion that there was one God and one God alone in all the universe. This God, the Aton, "loved all men equally" and was a God of peace (Payne,1964). Unlike what happened in the worship of Amon-Ra,

> "No image of the god was hidden away, to be bathed, annointed, dressed and fed each day. There were no statues or images of the Aton."

He was only symbolized by a painting or carving of the sun, from which rays descended earthward, each ray ending in a hand or "ankh", the Egyptian symbol of life.

The worship was not much different from today's. A choir sang and harpists played. A simple offering of flowers and fruits was placed upon a high altar. Hands were raised during worship to the healing rays of the sun. In Malachi 4:2, we read:

> "But to you who fear My name
> The Sun of Righteousness shall arise
> With healing in His wings;" (or rays).

The reference to the "Sun of Righteousness" obviously refers to Jesus Christ. It is also obvious here that it was not the sun, per se, which they worshipped but the God Almighty whose symbol was the sun.

This concept of God as one who loved all people equally reminds us of our understanding of God today. For Akhnaton, there was no room in his religious philosophy for war and violence. Only the disclosure of the Father through the Son, Jesus Christ, reminds us of this view of the God of love Who is no "respecter" of persons.

Unlike "Ra" whom the earlier priests had recognized as God and who had priests that worshipped in the temple and in the Holy of Holies; and whose symbol was the disc of the sun, and who was said to have actually led Thutmose III (1484-1461BC) to victory over the Assyrians in the very first recorded battle by archeologists, Aton was recognized as the only God worthy of worship.

This attempt at reform by Ahknaton and his queen Nefertiti, did not outlive the short life of this Pharaoh. Ancient Egypt went back to the worship of their many gods while including God the Almighty; hence God's ultimate plan to establish a people for Himself as a means of blessing all nations through Abraham.

The late Sir Wallis Budge, in his book Egyptian Religion, gives us some ideas and concepts, which date back to ancient Egypt but sound very familiar to those who know the scriptures. Reference has been made earlier to the possible origin of the concept of the Trinity: Father, Son and Holy Spirit. We are told that "Ra" (the sun), became the visible type and symbol of God, and that as far back as the fourth dynasty (about 3,700 BC), He (Ra) was regarded as the great God of heaven, and the king of all the gods, and divine beings, and the beatified dead who dwelt therein.

> "The position of the beatified in heaven is decided by Ra; and of all the gods there, Osiris only appears to have the power to claim protection for his followers; the offerings which the deceased would make to Ra are actually presented to Him by Osiris" (ibid.46).

Osiris the prototype of Jesus Christ, reminds us of Jesus presenting our offerings to God the Father, and how He is our advocate Who intercedes for us according to Hebrews and 1 John 2 (1-2). The Egyptian's hope at one time was to become God, the son of God by adoption, and that Ra would actually become his father. (Here also we see how we have been adopted into the kingdom of God).

The One, Self-begotten, and Self-existent God whom the Egyptians worshipped was associated with the sun—Ra. He was the Power of Powers as mentioned earlier. He was the everlasting creator, and was adored as such, not as the sun, per se, when it sets in the heavens. It was He who made the generations of men to flourish through the Nile-flood, and who caused gladness to exist in all lands, cities, and temples (Ibid,60).

Reference has been made to Osiris as the prototype of Jesus. Jesus said: "I am the Alpha and the Omega, The Beginning and the End,…Who is and Who was and Who is to come, the Almighty" (Rev.1:8). From the mapping of the Zodiac through concepts of "Ra" and beliefs about "Osiris" as god of the underworld, and the presence of the Holy Spirit throughout Old Testament times to the coming of Jesus Christ, one could confirm that He not only is, but was and is to come. Jesus was the true fulfillment of all previous revelations. It follows then that no religion or even a "Christian" denomination is complete when Jesus Christ is not the center and focus of attention.

Jesus Christ came to fulfill God's plan and purposes for the world. The major purpose was to redeem mankind from the deception of Satan with consequent spiritual separation from God. The purpose of the antagonist, Satan, was to destroy or distort God's works and plans for his children. Jesus, the protagonist, came to restore mankind back to God's original plans and purposes, and His victory had been assured

"I AM NOT COME TO DESTROY, BUT TO FULFIL" (Mt. 5:17b)

from the blueprint. We know the outcome was to be victory for Jesus and His people. The interesting thing is that this blueprint is still unfolding until the second coming of Jesus and His final victory over Satan. But what the Lord has fulfilled so far spans all the prophecies found in the Bible as well as those set down from the foundation of the earth.

To the unbeliever, the question is whether Jesus is still alive. To be told that Jesus is alive simply doesn't seem to make sense until one has come to a personal experience of Him. If He is alive we need to hear His own testimony. We have such testimony in Revelations when Jesus showed Himself to John on the island of Patmos. He said to John:

> "I am the Alpha and the Omega", says the Lord God, "who is and who was, and who is coming, the All-Sovereign". (We are reminded of Taurus, the rampaging bull in the Zodiac blueprint.) "When I saw Him I fell at His feet as dead. Then He laid His right hand on me and said, "Do not fear. I am the First and the Last and the Living One. I experienced death, and behold, I am alive forever and ever, and I possess the keys of death and of its realm" (Re.1:8, 17-18 MLB).

Reference has been made to how Jesus was exalted. Here we will briefly expound on how He achieved that authority; how He achieved the vastness of His authority so that

> "at the name of Jesus every knee should bow, of those in heaven, and of those on earth, and of those under the earth, and every tongue should confess that Jesus Christ is Lord, to the glory of God the Father (Ph.2:10-11).

In a teaching by Kenneth Copeland on the "Authority of the Believer" he explained that Jesus gained His authority over Satan in three ways: He inherited it; it was conferred on Him; He gained it by conquest. First He gained it through inheritance.

> "God…has in these last days spoken to us by His Son, whom He has appointed heir of all things, through whom He made the world;… (Heb.1:2).

Jesus inherited that authority but it was also conferred on Him after He fulfilled the Father's will and was obedient unto death. In death He conquered and stripped Satan of his power and authority over man and took from him the keys of death.

> "Having disarmed principalities and powers, He made a public spectacle of them, triumphing over them in it" (Col.2:15).

He was raised from the dead and achieved His authority ultimately by conquest as established in the Zodiac. After His resurrection from the dead and before He ascended to heaven he told His disciples:

> "All authority has been given to Me in heaven and on earth,
> Go therefore and make disciples of all the nations, baptizing them in the name of the Father and of the Son and of the Holy Spirit, teaching them to observe all things that I have commanded you;…" (Mt.28:19-20).

Mark 16:17 also adds:

> "And these signs will follow those who believe: In My name they will cast out demons; they will speak with new tongues; they will take up serpents; and if they drink anything deadly, it will by no means hurt them; they will lay hands on the sick, and they will recover."

It was on the basis of this command that the apostle Peter said to the lame man at the beautiful gate:

> "Silver and gold I do not have, but what I do have I give you:
> In the name of Jesus Christ of Nazareth, rise up and walk"
> (Acts 3:6).

It is this same authority which Christians are supposed to use and which many have been using ever since. If Christians are not operating in this power, we understand that it is because they are not walking in faith which works through love (Ga.5:6).

To the question, "Is He alive?" the answer is a resounding "Yes!". He is alive. He is the Alpha and Omega, the beginning and the ending. He is, He was, and He is coming. He lives in the present through the Holy Spirit who does the work of healing and restoration in a Benny Hinn crusade. He gives "word of knowledge" in healing and of things in the lives of people both past, present and future, when He reveals to His anointed one information that baffles the scientist.

At a crusade in Sydney, Australia, a woman was healed and was brought onto the stage when Benny Hinn asked her: "Are you Indian?" The woman responded "Yes". The Pastor continued: "Your forefathers, two generations ago, were involved in the occult". The woman agreed. It was the result of that bondage from which she was being released. On another person's hand covered by a long sleeves-shirt, the Holy Spirit revealed to Pastor Hinn that there were bruises like snakebites. He asked her to pull off the sleeves, and to the amazement of everyone, the bruises were there.

Another person in his fifties came and he was told that he used to be enthusiastic in the work of God when he was in his twenties and was asked why he did not continue. These are examples of word of knowledge. How does science explain this?

When a disease like cancer wreaks havoc on the lives of individuals, and to the medical profession, there seems to be no hope, Jesus shows up through the Holy Spirit and grants instant healing to the sick. This healing is effected regardless of whether the one is a doctor himself or not, as happened to a medical doctor who traveled to one such crusade in Puerto Rico. He was instantly healed of a prostate cancer in its last stages. The doctors gave up on this colleague of theirs but Jesus healed him instantly and that doctor is presently volunteering his time to help out in other crusades.

In one case Jesus showed Himself to the one being healed. This happened in Melbourne, Australia, when a man who was given one day to live because of liver failure, checked himself out of the hospital and came to a crusade. Jesus told Benny Hinn that He was giving him a brand new liver. A few seconds later Jesus showed Himself to the man as Benny pointed his finger upwards at an angle of about forty five degrees and asked the man: "What do you see?" He screamed "I see Jesus! I see Jesus!" before being "slain in the spirit", or falling under the anointing. Do we need more evidence?

In a book by Benny Hinn: "Lord, I need a Miracle" (1993), he cites case after case of healing documented by medical doctors. But there are numerous cases not even reported. One such first hand experience concerns a friend who was healed of Multiple sclerosis. She had been in a wheel chair for over eight months. We used to carry her with the wheel chair or simply wheeled her around. It was a very cold winter day in February 1993, and we drove her to Philadelphia, believing the Lord would heal her. We were in the overflow the first day and nothing happened. We got into the major auditorium early on Friday. Just about twenty minutes into the praise and worship service, I heard some commotion in her area. To my amazement, she came out of the wheel chair and started walking, even running! It has been eight years now and she has kept her healing, by the grace of God.

In the process of such encounters with the Spirit of God, many report that an electric shock passed through their bodies, or they experience heat, or a burning sensation. Some report a kind of breeze around them or simply an experience of being engulfed by the love of God. Sometimes a word of knowledge from God calls the kind of healing taking place simultaneously as the healing occurs.

These are but samples of the numerous words of knowledge and healing that take place; some in the past but also going on today, in the ministries of many other pastors and of evangelists such as Oral Roberts, Smith Wigglesworth or Yogi Cho, across cultures and throughout history. Jesus is the same yesterday, today and forever, pictured in the

Zodiac, who entered human history, died and came back to life and continues forever and ever on earth through the Holy Spirit. He is the same, we are told, and is coming back according to God's plan, which is still unfolding. The more we understand about the roots of our faith, the easier it is for us to connect whatever is happening as all part of His original plan and purpose which Satan can never destroy because it is forever settled in heaven.

Satan is not only a liar but a deceiver. He is called the god of this world and we are told that he blinds the minds of people from seeing the truth (2Cor4:4). Elsewhere in Romans 1:18,22) we are told of

> "men who suppress the truth in unrighteousness" (and)
> "Professing to be wise they became fools".

One of his tricks successfully used to date is to cut Christians from their roots.

Our next chapter will attempt to bring out some reasons why the enemy has so far succeeded in making Christians even ashamed to connect with their roots in ancient Egypt.

7

ARE CHRISTIANS ASHAMED OF THEIR ROOTS?

Jesus said: "I am the Way, the Truth and the Life". He also said: "And you will know the Truth, and the Truth shall set you free" (John 8:32).

It is only the truth we know that will set us free from bondage but the Truth also refers to Jesus. When we truly know Him we are set free from the bondage of racial prejudice, and become truly free.

In this chapter, we will attempt to establish that the god of this world, Satan, has blinded not only the whole world from seeing the truth about the glorious gospel of Jesus Christ as the redeemer (II Cor. 4:4). He has also blinded many Christians who ordinarily would have nothing to do with the enemy, to accept the lie of racial theories and their consequences of man's inhumanity to man.

The Church went along to support slavery, which was Satan's devise for economic gain for those who, using the theory of evolution, established themselves as superior to those being enslaved. The Catholic Church was said to have signed "The Asiento" or contract of 1713 to allow Britain to export slaves to the Spanish colonies in South America.

"The Church became the primary moral sanctioner for the brutal institution of slave trading" (Asante& Mattson,1992:24).

She also accepted compensation based on the number of slaves exported.

The Trans-Atlantic slave trade was said to have started in 1517, after Bishop Bartholomew De Las Casas, became an eye witness of the atrocities committed by the Spanish Christians in Mexico. They were reported to have burned alive the Indian chiefs and reduced a teeming population of twenty five million to only one million because they would not convert to Christianity. De Las Casas was said to have recommended to Pope Leo X who issued an order for the importation of Africans to replace the exterminated Native Americans (Ofiaja APM, Vol.5 No.1, 2000).

This was followed by the institution of colonialism with the same motive of economic gain at the expense of those considered inferior.

Why was the Church, supposed to be light to the world, involved in this trade? She obviously accepted the lie of the enemy through the theory of evolution and the love of money, which is Satan's bait and chief weapon for running this world. Obviously the Church bought into racial theories which derived from the theory of evolution.

The theory of evolution states among others, that

> "The evolutionary history of the world from the 'big bang' to the present universe, is a series of gradual steps from the simple to the complicated, from the unordered to the organized..." (Morris 2000, 21. Cited from Weisskopf, 1977)*

Dr Morris points out that this unscientific notion that higher degrees of organized complexity can suddenly emerge out of a chaotic milieu completely contradicts

> "the second law of thermodynamics, which stipulates that all real systems and processes tend naturally to deteriorate to greater randomness...to lower degrees of organization and complexity..." (ibid., 129).

In other words, all things tend to degenerate and decay with age rather than improve in quality. But as a result of this faulty evolutionary foundation, God had been ruled out as Creator, (contrary to the ancient Egyptians' view of the world). There is no need for God in any portion of the comprehensive evolutionary scenario, observes Dr. Morris.

> "If everything from the universe itself to man has evolved by natural processes from the primeval chaos (or nothingness) into their present complex forms and relationships, God becomes quite redundant" (ibid.,22).

Phillip Johnson, author of "Darwin on Trial" in "Defeating Darwinism by Opening Minds" quotes from the "famous Harvard geneticist Richard Lewontin, one of the most influential biologists in the world" who wrote:

> "Moreover, that materialism is absolute, for we cannot allow a Divine Foot in the door[1]...To appeal to an Omnipotent deity is to allow that at any moment the regularities of nature may be ruptured, that miracles may happen" (Johnson 1997, 81; quoting from Lewontin)

Phillip Johnson explains:

> "Evolution is not a fact, it's a philosophy". He continues:
> "To a materialist, putting up with any amount of bad practice in science is better than to let that Divine Foot in the door." (ibid.)

Evolution became the worldview that permeated and controlled all disciplines. Dr. David Jeremiah writes of evolutionary theory:

---

1. The truth is that the "Divine Foot" which materialism refuses to allow in the door is a regular presence at a Benny Hinn crusade where the "regularities of nature are ruptured" when a cancer or other illnesses are healed.

> "Many layers of error have been built on the faulty foundation of evolution. Humanism is the natural result. If God is not central in all our thinking, then man must be. Atheism is humanism's twin brother, and consistent evolutionists cannot logically believe in the personal God of the Bible, the God who is the Creator of all life. Abortion, infanticide, and euthanasia are logical behaviors for those who have so easily disposed of the image of God in the eternal soul of man. The concept of a resurrected body and eternal life is also a casualty of this evil philosophy...Pornography, adultery, divorce, homosexuality, premarital sex, the destruction of the nuclear family—all are weeds that have grown from Satan's big lie about the universe.... Satan and his evolutionary gospel hate God as the Creator, Christ as the Savior, and the Bible as the Word of God. Modern evolutionism is simply the continuation of Satan's long war against God (Morris 2000,10).

We are reminded of Romans (2:28-31), which identifies some of these same kinds of behavior when we reject God from our knowledge. We have a similar behavior listed in Galatians (5:19-22) when the flesh is in control rather than the spirit.

A few examples will document how this faulty thinking promoted systems such as racism, militarism, imperialism, and finally reached their zenith in Nazi Germany under Adolf Hitler (ibid.,75).

Racism emerged from the view that

> "all races had gone through a mammalian stage shortly before birth. The various stages of the Caucasian childhood are said to represent the various lower races and their attainments—with the blacks at the bottom, then the yellow races, and whites at the top" (ibid.,62).

The standard of intelligence of the average adult Negro was said to be similar to that of the eleven-year-old youth of the Homo sapiens, according to this "highly educated Scientist who did not believe in the Bible" (ibid.).

A fundamental offshoot of evolutionary theory was "survival of the fittest". Some of the forerunners employing this perspective included one of the "Founding Fathers" of sociology, Herbert Spencer. He argued for a survival-of-the-fittest philosophy. He wrote:

> "Fostering the good-for-nothing at the expense of the good, is an extreme cruelty...There is no greater curse to posterity than that of bequeathing to them an increasing population of imbeciles and idlers and criminals...The whole effort of nature is to get rid of such, to clear the world of them and make room for better...If they are not complete to live, they die and it is best they should die" (Spencer, cited in Abrams 1968,74; as quoted by Ritzer,1996).

Andrew Carnegie was one of his admired sponsors and it is obvious why Spencer would support Laissez-faire capitalism that would enrich the industrialist-sponsors but seek to get rid of the poor and "good-for-nothing".

Since the Caucasian race chose to assign itself the top of the evolutionary ladder rather than the ancient Egyptians who were black, they also allocated themselves the responsibility of what they called the "White man's burden"[2] which was a pretext for imperialism. This meant that they were responsible for taking care of those considered inferior through the institution of colonialism and imperialism.

With reference to America,

> "The Darwinian mood sustained the belief in Anglo-Saxon racial superiority which obsessed many American thinkers in the latter half of the nineteenth century. The measure of world dominion already achieved by the 'race' seemed to prove it the fittest" Hofstader, Social Darwinism, 172-3, cited by Morris 2000,70).

---

2. Evolutionary theory rejected the concept that man is created in God's image: "And He has made from one blood every nation of men..." (Acts17:26). Hierarchies of men were created and the White assigned the top position and the so-called responsibility for others especially Blacks.

The concept of "manifest destiny"[3] which was a kind of divine approval to take over the land from Native Americans also stemmed from this perspective.

In Germany, Hitler applied this evolutionary theory when in "Mein Kampf (My Struggle), using the same concept of survival of the fittest, he wrote:

> "The noblest of all human stocks was the Nordic race. The Jews formed a subhuman counter race, predestined by their biological heritage to evil, just as the Nordic race was designated for nobility…A radiant future would beckon to a world redeemed by the Aryan spirit, liberated from the 'Jewish World Poisoners', and also from the shackles of Judaic-descended Christianity" (Cited in Gann, Adolf Hitler, quoted by Morris 2000, 78).

But it was not only Jews that Hitler persecuted.

> "He opposed and persecuted Christians–both Catholic and Protestant–as well as Jews, blacks, gypsies, and other 'inferiors' (ibid.).

For Hitler, evolution was the Hallmark of modern science and culture. He was only implementing what the theorists such as Spencer had argued that

> "If they are not sufficiently complete to live, they die, and it is best they should die".

It was when Hitler carried out this theoretical suggestion in connection with the Jews, that racism as a theory came out of favor.

> "The military collapse of Germany and the unveiling of the death camps prompted a universal revulsion of the intelligentsia against

---

3. In American history "manifest destiny" implies divine sanction for U.S. territorial expansion. It was coined in 1845 based on the same concept of the White Man's burden, in this case with reference to Native Americans.

the intellectual traditions that had contributed to Nazi ideology, foremost among them the notion of a hierarchical subordination of human populations" (ibid.,75 cited from Matt et al,).[4]

It is worth noting that racial theories did not become unpopular until it was applied by Hitler to the Jewish people during World War II. Even long after that, racism continued as far as Blacks were concerned. It was especially alive in the United States and South Africa under apartheid where the white minority oppressed the majority Blacks.

In America, where the founding fathers wrote: "We hold these truths to be self-evident that all men are created equal...", Blacks still went through four centuries of the institution of slavery followed by over one hundred years of virtual slavery until the 1960s of the Civil Rights Movement. Here we are impressed by the Nazi-type police brutality of Mississippi and Selma or Montgomery, Alabama with the police dogs, bombings, fire hoses, jailing, killing of Civil rights leaders and all those supporting them including children. These also remind us of White rule in South Africa under apartheid with mass killing of freedom fighters such as the mass killings in Sharpville and Soweto[5] and imprisonment of leaders like Nelson Mandella who became the first president after the dissolution of the apartheid machinery.

We still hear a whole lot about concentration camps and the atrocities of Hitler in Nazi Germany, but very little about what happened to Blacks over the centuries of brutality, injustice and man's inhumanity to man based on a false philosophy.

The theory of evolution, as noted, is a rejection of God as the Creator, as believed by the ancient Egyptians. The Greeks obtained their

---

4. Matt Cartmill, David Pilbeam, and Glynn Isaac, "One hundred years of Paleoanthropology," American Scientist (74 July/Aug.1986);418
5. Sharpville and Soweto in South Africa were two cities where peaceful demonstrations against Apartheid were met by mass shooting and killings by the police of both children and adults.

knowledge from ancient Egypt, as compellingly documented by George James (1978), but they failed to grasp the Egyptian teaching about God as the Creator in their belief system and that provided the foundation for evolutionary theory.

As a "scientific theory", as noted, it has no evidence and has been thoroughly discredited today by many scientists themselves. When asked for evidence of evolution they claim that the "best" evidence is "imperfections" found in nature which do not take into account the fact of deterioration, or the fact that God cursed the earth because of Satan (Morris, 2000).

Racial theories of superior and inferior races, as noted, not only resulted in such atrocities as the holocaust in Nazi Germany, but also explains the kind of chattel slavery which operated in America. It is still the basis of prejudice, discrimination, segregation and many other kinds of institutional privileges set up for the benefit of "whites" in this country.

The Church failed to be guided by Acts (17:26) which states:

> "From one man He made every nation of men, that they should inhabit the whole earth; and He determined the times set for them and the exact places where they should live." (NIV)

As the Church obviously went astray and followed the lies of Satan, she also used evolutionary theory to explain cultural and color differences which still serve as the foundation of racism today even within the Church.

Someone has suggested that rather than considering themselves as a religious, or a spiritual idea that God used to bless all nations, the Jewish people considered themselves an ethnic group with all that comes with ethnocentrism, national pride, and the development of the roots of race and racism. This meant the exclusion of others from the plans and purposes of God until Jesus finally came on the scene.

When the angels sang glory to God in the highest at the birth of Jesus, they also added "and on earth peace among men with whom He is well pleased" (Lk2:14).

His coming was to bring peace among men. It is beautiful to find believers worshipping together regardless of shades of color, national origin, language or culture. This is however, the exception and not the rule especially in America.

One may ask: Why did God create people with different shades of color so that one ethnic group considers itself better than the other? Did God actually create some people to be servants of others? The Bible says that God created man from the dust of the ground in His own image and likeness and breathed into him the breath of life (Ge.1:26;2:7). Scientists have now come to accept that all the elements found in man are also found in the dust of the earth. The Bible does not refer to any color differences in God's original creation but He has also built into the human genetic system an ability to adapt to his environment. Melanin in the human skin determines our skin color which in turn controls how much sunlight we need as this same melanin acts to block excessive sunlight with harmful rays from our body. This has resulted in about 2,000 shades of color in the human family, according to some scientists. The rich diversity in God's creation was for the benefit of man. But there is also the enemy of God, Satan, whose purpose as stated above, has been to distort or destroy the plan and purposes of God. God's beautiful human diversities Satan turned into something evil to turn one group against the other.

The leaders in the development of science were Christians who believed that they were "thinking God's thoughts after Him". God gave them the ideas; ideas that He had already established. But there also evolved a group that developed their own faith apart from God. That faith or philosophy called "evolution" excluded God from everything as mentioned above.

Social scientists, especially Sociologists and Anthropologists, were the chief culprits in the development of racial theories and the picture cannot be complete without reference to Count Arthur J. de Gobineau

(1816-1882). In "Essays on the Inequality of the human races", this father of modern racial theories, admitted that his purpose in writing was in part "to prove the superiority of his own race. He preached the superiority of the White race over the other races, and of the Aryans over all other whites" with the blacks, of course, being the lowest. He contended that every civilization had its origin from the Aryans. "The supreme race is the Aryan, and the Teutons are its purest modern representation". He claimed that "the Egyptian civilization was created by an Aryan colony from India; the Greek's was due to Aryans with some Semitic intermixture. Civilization without an Aryan creator is unthinkable" according to him, (Klineberg 1935,3).

Here we find how knowledge is distorted to suit ones preconceived ideas, similar to what materialists do as they accept bad practice in science rather than allow the Divine Foot in the door. He obviously did not know that the "blond Nordic peoples" were hunters and herdsmen "a lowly race" who saw little of the civilization in Egypt before 1500 BC (Payne, 1964).

Jesus tells us that Satan is a liar and the father of lies (John 8:44b). His intention is to distort everything that God created and here we find a good example. Color differences that were meant for human survival in different environments of the world, have been misinterpreted to mean that one color is superior to another. As a result of this kind of thinking, millions of Africans perished in the Trans-Atlantic slave trade while millions of Jews also perished in German concentration camps when Hitler sought to implement the "survival of the fittest" idea.

Not only has the theory of evolution been thoroughly discredited. Microbiologists have also recently come to concede that life at its irreducible base, consists of complex machines. This, of course, agrees with David's statement that we are fearfully and wonderfully made (Ps139:4). But without this understanding and wisdom from God, man is misled by Satan to believe lies, which hold him in bondage, even as "Christians".

What role does color prejudice play regarding the acceptance of the truth of the African roots of our faith? We have established that the ancient Egyptians carefully and laboriously mapped out the Zodiac, which is actually the gospel in the stars. We have also established that they knew God Almighty even though many other gods were acknowledged. We are told by Prof. Finch, that even if we were to yield to a more conservative reckoning (from the 10,000 BC. by Gerald Massey),[6]

> "it is clear that there is at least a 4,500-year connection that leads to Christianity out of Africa and through ancient Egypt or Kemit, (K'mt). It is this that we propose to explore because the evidence, carefully considered, begins to force upon one the conclusion that the Kamitic influence was the preponderant one, that what became historical Christianity was largely an elaboration and re-working of Kamitic religious and symbolic ideas" (Finch, in Saakana, Ed., 1988,33).

This is because God, the Creator who has no problem with color differences, because He created them, and is the same yesterday, today and forever, has shown Himself to the ancient Egyptians also. Jesus came to fulfill and not to destroy, except to destroy the works of the enemy, Satan. Prof. Finch goes on to explain that this is a long-buried truth that is shattering to some when brought to light.

> "This is undoubtedly an heretical and blasphemous idea to modern Christian divines but early on, canonical or 'official' Christianity buried great many truths under the blanket of 'heresy'". He continues:
> "To propose that Christianity was Kamitic in origin must seem to some to be turning Christianity upside down on its head; rather it is setting Christianity right side up on its feet" (ibid.).

---

6. Gerald Massey, in "Natural Genesis", is said to have traced the Christ concept back 10,000 years BC to the lands drained by the Nile River on the continent of Africa.

We only need to ask ourselves: Would Jesus prefer that we stay in ignorance concerning our roots, or would He welcome for us to know the truth which only will set us free? It is evident that racial prejudice is the only reason people find it difficult to accept this as true. We have conditioned our minds to accept lies from those who developed the racial theories and even now there are many so-called Christians who would not like "to be confused by the facts" because their minds are made up! There is racism in the Church; perhaps less so than elsewhere, but racism is there nonetheless. A Pastor of a large inner-city church said that while people of all colors do everything together—such as riding the buses and trains together, sharing wards in hospitals, playing basketball or even doing drugs together; Sunday at eleven o'clock is the most segregated hour of the week. At that time people segregate into their various churches, Blacks to Black churches, Whites to White churches while Hispanics go to Hispanic churches.

If the Church is unwilling to accept the truth about its very origin in ancient Egypt—because it is African—it would be difficult for the world to accept from her any teaching, especially, the truth about racial reconciliation that the Bible teaches about. We are also saying in effect, that it would be easier for us to accept as truth if the origin were to be from the Aryan race because they claim to be superior, and according to them, civilization without them is unthinkable.

It is fearful how difficult it is to change people's minds. God Himself found that the most difficult thing was to keep the Israelites from changing their minds from returning to slavery in Egypt. He had to lead them by the long way. The point is that it is easier for us to stay the way we are rather than attempt to change.

Many Christians would probably find it hard accepting the truth of the African origin of their faith. They are most likely ashamed of their roots the same way African-Americans have been taught, using the same racial theories, to be ashamed of Africa as their place of origin. After that mindset had been corrected, this shame was replaced by pride. Similarly, when Christians come to accept the truth of the African origin of their faith, many who reject Christianity as a "White man's religion" will most likely come to receive the Lord as their personal savior. Problems of racism, discrimination and segregation might also have a better chance at solution.

Another factor that might have contributed to the disregard of ancient Egypt as the source of our faith was the way the Egyptians were perceived when God pulled out His people after 430 years from Egyptian bondage. It was in fulfillment of His original promise He made to Abraham whom God promised to bless so he would be a blessing to all nations (Ge.12:2-3). As noted above, the very idea of Israel was to be a religious, a spiritual idea. It was not because they were any special except that God wanted to train and purify them so that through them He would establish a people for Himself through whom He would send His Son Jesus Christ.

We need not see the Hebrews set against the Egyptians, as one race against the other, but as the Power of God against the power of Satan. The only thing that separated them from their brother Egyptians was because of God's own plan to show His superiority and ascendancy over the powers of all the other gods that were worshipped in ancient Egypt despite the fact that at least some knew and worshipped Him. The phrase: "That they may know that I am God Almighty" has been repeated many times, and God often used it to justify His wonderful miracles on behalf of the Hebrews. God also says of Himself "I am a jealous God" and "My Name is Jealous" (Ex.20:5, 34:14).

Instead of viewing themselves as God's means of reaching the whole world, they focused more on themselves as a nationalist group, with special favors from God. It is true that God actually showed them special favors as He helped them not only against the Egyptians but also against all the ethnic groups that were previously on the land of Canaan. God used them to wipe out and punish those people because of their sins against Him. Like the Canaanites, the Egyptians found themselves in the enemy's camp and God was basically dealing with Satan so anyone who aligned himself with Satan came under God's judgement. This also explains why God punished Israel herself at times of disobedience. Whenever sin was committed, they were punished as in the case of Achan whose greed led him to take some of the spoils after they had been warned not to do so by Joshua. This led to a sound defeat by a small group of the people of Ai. As soon as they confessed their sins as a nation they were able to defeat their enemies (Joshua 7-8). The point is that God was not necessarily concerned with them as a separate ethnic group of people with special favors just because they were descendants of Abraham as they thought. For God is no respecter of persons. He is respecter of faith and obedience to Him. Even though it all started with Israel, the goal was to reach all mankind through Jesus Christ. This was why it was so difficult for the Jews later on to understand what Jesus was trying to do. They claimed to be Abraham's seed but Jesus told them:

> "You are of your father the devil, and the desires of your father you want to do" (John8:44a).

We see the same focus on themselves as a people, the reason why they found it hard to accept other ethnic groups even though God has specifically told them to make a place for the aliens. After they came back from captivity, they were to divide the land by lot

> "as an inheritance for yourselves, and for the strangers who sojourn among you and who bear children among you...in whatever tribe the stranger sojourns, there you shall give him his inheritance." (Ezekiel:22a,23).

They also found it difficult to accept the Samaritans who were also Jews but intermarried with other ethnic groups. There was a wall of separation between Jews and Gentiles and God had to send the apostles Paul and Peter to break down those walls through the preaching of the gospel. When the Holy Spirit fell on the Gentiles just as He had fallen on the Jews at Pentecost and Peter baptized the house of Cornelius, he had to defend his action to the assembly in Jerusalem.

> "When they heard these things they became silent; and they glorified God, saying, 'Then God has also granted to the Gentiles repentance to life'" (Acts 11:18).

It was hard for the Jews to accept that the Gentiles were equally acceptable to God.

With this sense of nationalism in view of being chosen by God, they probably forgot God's real intention to bless all nations through them. Ancient Egypt herself was regarded as an enemy because of God's dealings with the Pharaoh who opposed Him. It would seem obvious why they would truncate themselves from Egyptian roots because they considered the Egyptians their enemies rather than see them as those who aligned with Satan through their leader. That was the same reason God forbade them from returning there or worshipping the many gods apart from the Lord God Almighty. It was not because of their color or nationality.

When Jesus came, it was not only to reconcile God to man but also man to man. In His own background was Gentile blood and He is presented as a universal person who has broken down the "middle wall of division between us" [Jew and Gentile] (Lk.2:14). All are one in the Lord regardless of race, color, nationality, gender, or even position in life.

In conclusion, as Prof. Finch has noted, Christianity is being set right side up on its feet when it acknowledges its true source of origin from the cradle of civilization. They have been the first to recognize Jesus Christ in the stars when they laboriously and painstakingly mapped out the Zodiac. They were also the first to give us our ideas and concepts about God, which have rarely changed over the years. It was this same Jesus who said, "I am the Way, the Truth and the Life", as we shall examine in more detail in our next chapter.

8

"I AM THE WAY, THE TRUTH AND THE LIFE"
(John 14:6)

In this modern world of relativism where everything is considered of equal value, the claim on the part of Jesus Christ to be "The Way, the Truth and the Life" is considered bigoted and narrow minded for any one to believe it. Those same people will, however, consider it unsafe for anyone else to suggest a path to the moon other than those planned by the scientists for astronauts. But following the same reasoning one could say it is narrow minded on the part of the scientists to plan only one specific path, together with mid-course corrections, to reach the destination. The Creator Himself has said "this is the Way...walk ye in it" and yet man chooses to doubt it. Jeremiah said:

"O Lord, I know the way of man is not in himself;
It is not in man who walks to direct his own steps" (Jer.10:23).

Psalm 37:23 assures us:

"The steps of a good man are ordered by the Lord".

A review of the discussion so far suggests that it is more reasonable to believe the Creator of the Universe than the scientist, who only depends on physical laws established by God in the first place, even if he disowns Him.

Those who mapped out the Zodiac had established that two forces had been at work since creation. These forces are good and evil; positive and negative; light and darkness; life and death; God and Satan. Right there also, the Creator had established the winner of the contest in the person of Jesus Christ.

Lucifer, later as Satan, had been cast out of heaven before man came on the scene. Satan managed to convince man to disobey God and so man lost his special place and protection by God. He also lost his position as the owner of this world over which he was supposed to have dominion. Satan got the ownership and even suggested to give its authority and glory to Jesus if only He would bow down and worship him

> "for this has been delivered to me, and I give it to whomever I wish" (Luke4:6b).

Jesus did not question it but only commanded Satan to get behind Him. Satan became the god of this world even though God was still in control and Satan had to act under the authority of God as when he was allowed to test Job but with the condition not to touch his life.

Two camps or kingdoms had been established governed by two laws. One is the law of the Spirit of life in Christ Jesus and the other is the law of sin and death. When man is born he automatically comes under the curse. His nature and bent is toward evil. The self is the number one priority and it is especially strong in a baby. The self and its desires or lusts of the flesh is something that the spirit nature has to contend with to overcome. The self has its needs and contends for them to be satisfied, but they are often contrary to the direction of the spirit. The soul, (mind or consciousness), is usually pulled along by the flesh. The Spirit of God comes in to reside in the body after salvation. He takes control of one's spirit, but the Word of God has to be consciously used to renew the mind so that it does not conform to the old nature and ways of doing things, but rather is transformed to align with the Word of God. Jesus said:

"It is the Spirit who gives life; the flesh profits nothing" (John 6:63).

The law of sin and death in Satan's kingdom operates when we walk according to the flesh with condemnation implied. It is not so for those who do not walk according to the dictates of the flesh, (Rom.8:1). Satan's example to his followers has been the way of rebellion and that which does not retain God in its knowledge. God gives up one to a debased mind, which in turn leads to all kinds of sin along the lines of debased human nature. This was what happened when evolutionary theory took over as mentioned above. Paul gives us a listing of them in Rom.1:28-31:

> Furthermore, since they did not think it worthwhile to retain the knowledge of God, He gave them over to a depraved mind, to do what ought not to be done. They have become filled with every kind of wickedness, evil, greed and depravity. They are full of envy, murder, strife, deceit and malice. They are gossips, slanderers, God-haters, insolent, arrogant and boastful; they invent ways of doing evil; they disobey their parents; they are senseless, faithless, heartless, ruthless (NIV).

We find a similar listing of all kinds of sin imaginable when the flesh is allowed to be in control. This is found in Galatians (5:19-22) when sinful nature takes over control from the spirit nature.

Unlike the enemy, the example of Jesus has been that of obedience and submission to the Father's will. He often said that He came not to do His own will, but the Father's. Unlike Satan's kingdom, the kingdom of God operates by the law of the Spirit of life in Christ Jesus (the anointed and in His anointing). It operates by "faith working through love" (Ga.5:6b). Faith connects us to the anointing of Jesus Christ who is the Jubilee that frees man from every kind of bondage. Faith in His Word when He said in Luke (4:18) that the Spirit of the Lord was upon Him and that He was anointed to preach the gospel to the poor,...to heal the broken hearted; to preach deliverance to the captives, and recovery of sight to the blind; and to set at liberty those who are oppressed, as noted above. This is the good news or the gospel, and only faith in Him connects one to it. He said to the woman with the issue of blood: "Your faith has made you whole." She was the only one who could connect by faith, which drew upon the anointing for her to receive her healing. Similarly, Jesus saw the faith of the men who passed their sick friend through the opening in the ceiling. Even though there was power or the anointing available to heal everyone who would draw upon it, only that man's faith pulled on the anointing to receive his healing (Luke 5:20).

Jesus taught that faith works only through love. The only commandment He gave His disciples, and to all who would follow Him, was to love one another (John15:12). Love, we are also told elsewhere, covers a multitude of sins. In this kingdom ruled by God the Father, God the Son, and God the Holy Spirit, the law of the spirit of life works to redeem or reclaim man back to God's original purpose for him; namely, that of fellowship with Him to enjoy Him forever. Unlike the devil's kingdom where death reigns because of sin, life rules here. Jesus said that by their fruits you will know them. Here we experience the fruit of the Spirit, which are love, joy, peace, long suffering, kindness, goodness, faithfulness, gentleness, and self-control. This is achieved when the Word of God is allowed to transform the mind so that the human spirit takes control from the flesh which we are told should be mortified or put to death. Self discipline is essential in this for man to reach anywhere near the potential of the stature of Jesus Christ. The goal of growth for the Christian through the work of the apostles, prophets, evangelists, pastors and teachers is:

> "for the equipping of the saints for the work of ministry, for the edifying of the body of Christ, till we all come to the unity of the faith and the knowledge of the Son of God to a **perfect man, to the measure of the stature of the fullness of Christ**" (Eph.4:11-13).

If, as mentioned above, there are only two kingdoms: that of good and evil; life and death; light and darkness; God and Satan; and God had actually established this from the foundation of creation, it would follow that there could only be two ways and two choices. Man cannot but participate in the choice between these two kingdoms. He is actually born into one and has to make a decision to be "born again" into the other. Man is born into Satan's kingdom even when his own parents are in the kingdom of God. He has to use his own will, as he hears the Word, to make a decision for God.

The god of this world is very powerful and his offers are very tempting. Just as he did in the Garden of Eden, he contradicts the Word of God and suggests that man can do better for himself; that he is in charge of his life. Money is often used as a powerful bait to promise happiness, fame and power; and abundant pleasures are promised. Jesus called someone a fool who considered his abundant harvest and told himself to take it easy and enjoy when his soul was actually required of him that very night. Satan focuses man's attention on the things of this world to the point that man forgets that life is not only this side of the grave. He often experiences a rude awakening when the end comes and it is often too late. Satan who is called the father of lies, as the god of this world, blinds man from seeing the truth about Jesus Christ as the light of the world and the source of life. He uses

> "principalities and powers; rulers of the darkness of this age; and spiritual hosts of wickedness in the heavenly places" (Ep.6:12).

Satan is known by his fruits, and some of them include experiences of degradation, shame, humiliation, suffering and pain, sickness and death. This is often what happens when man rejects God's direction for his life and decides to take control by himself. Not only the individual but a society that seeks its own way also suffers. When man is made the measure and not God, society decays; corrodes and falls from within. It is not so when God the Creator, through the Son Jesus Christ, is put in charge.

As Christians follow the example of their Master, Jesus Christ, there is obedience to the Father through the direction of the Word. The mind is transformed and the body comes under discipline and control. Since it is only the Spirit of God who gives life, physical life is often given back to individuals through miracle healing. There is much more that the human mind cannot comprehend which only the power of God can do. When the Divine Foot is allowed into the door, "the regularities of nature are often ruptured" and miracles do happen. When faith working by love, connects with the anointing of Jesus Christ, the impossible becomes possible. Reference has been made to miracles, word of knowledge, and salvation when God brings individuals out of the kingdom of Satan into the kingdom of God. Individuals who have been oppressed by the devil in many diverse ways whether through drugs, alcohol, suffering from diseases of every kind; this kingdom of God has power over all. Satan's power bows before God as Jesus resurrected from the dead and took the keys of death and hell from him.

In conclusion, when Jesus says: "I am the Way, the Truth and the Life" and that no man comes to the father except through Him, all the evidence points to the truth of that statement when there are only two kingdoms and two kings. He, the Son, is in charge of God's kingdom because everything has been committed to Him by the Father. The Holy Spirit, the third person in the trinity, has been at work bringing people to the kingdom through the preaching of the Word, while at the same time helping the people of God to grow in the things of God. We are told:

> "For there is one God, and one Mediator between God and men, the Man, Christ Jesus" (I Tim.2:5). In Acts 4:12 we also read:
> "Nor is there salvation in any other, for there is no other name under heaven given among men by which we must be saved."

Since He is in charge and in command in His kingdom, only He can show us how to come in to the Father through the Son. Any other way is a lie of the enemy and can never bring us to the kingdom. We only remain in the kingdom into which all men are born, the kingdom of Satan.

In our final chapter, we will briefly summarize, arrive at some conclusions and their implications for public school education in America.

9

SUMMARY, CONCLUSIONS, AND SOME IMPLICATIONS

In our concluding chapter, we will attempt to summarize some of the main points; make some conclusions and also point out a few implications with specific reference to American Public School Education.

The story of Ancient Egypt helps us understand that there was no civilization comparable to that of Egypt at the time. This was obvious to Herodotus during his visit. We are told that at a time when the ancestors of Western Europe still lived as "semi-savages in the dense forests of England and Europe" (Payne, 1964) a great civilization had thrived along the Nile Valley that had lasted for over 2,000 years before Christ. The pyramid of Giza had been constructed in addition to many wonderful developments.

Some writers maintain that such pyramids had been built through the slave labor of the Hebrews. Prof. Ben-Jochannan has summarized the achievements of the Native Africans of the Nile Valley, before "starvation brought Israel and his children, seventy in all, to ancient Egypt" when Joseph was the "Prime Minister" second only to Pharaoh.

These included proficiency in the sciences which enabled them to embalm their dead; name the bodies in the celestial universe; name their God and minor gods; develop agriculture; establish a solar calendar in 4,100BC; build temples to the Gods–including the world-wonder Sphinx of Gezer (Giza). Other developments included engineering;

medicine, including internal surgery; and pharmacology, among others, in addition to such disciplines as the writing of short stories.

Aside from those mentioned by Prof. Ben-Jochannan, reference has been made to Prof. George James' work quoted by Prof. Asa Hilliard. He asked some rhetorical questions which give us the context of developments that formed the bedrock of Christian faith in ancient Egypt. Much of this has been credited to Greece but the evidence proves just the contrary. These developments were also by those the "father of History" Herodotus described as, "burnt skinned, flat nosed, thick lipped, and wooly haired" (James:1976,Intro).

Our question of investigation has been whether Christianity, with the Bible, is a Western religion or African in origin? The preponderance of the evidence indicates that the Zodiac was mapped out in Egypt. It was called the "gospel in the skies" and it depicted the conflict between God and Satan with Jesus, the Seed of the woman, from Virgo to Leo, being depicted as the victor who is not only coming back to receive His own but also returning as a judge.

Where did these savant astronomer-priests obtain their information? Based on the general enlightenment of the time, we can deduce that they obtained it from their laborious studies and observations of the heavens. Revelation knowledge most likely played a part in it as well as the wealth of information from the "dateless past" when the accumulated written and oral literature were developed.

Much of the information from the astronomer-priests was recorded in the Book of the dead (Budge,1959). The concept of "dateless past..." rather than simply "In the beginning..." as Benny Hinn explains is the actual translation of the Hebrew (Ge.1:1), makes provision for some level of evolution as evidenced in various forms of adaptation but does not exclude God Almighty as the Creator. God initiated and created everything as the ancient Egyptians acknowledged but which their Greek students (James,1976) failed to include in their understanding. The evidence suggests that God created everything perfect but Lucifer's rebellion created chaos and destruction and that "evolution" and various forms of adaptation were used by God to salvage the situation.

It is important to recognize that Moses, who was highly educated in the wisdom of the Egyptians and groomed to become the next Pharaoh, had access to all that was rich in their literature in addition to God's personal revelation to him.

The concepts held by the ancient Egyptians of God, Satan and of Man have not very much changed from what we hold today. It was only when Jesus Christ came to fulfill the laws and the prophets by extending our understanding of God's intent and purposes behind them, that the dimension of love was demonstrated. Even here reference was made to Ahknaton who attempted to establish monotheism during his short reign. He concluded that God, the Aton, loved all men equally and was a God of peace. As such he was not engaged in warfare to maintain his empire.

It was only Jesus Christ,

> "who being the brightness of His glory and the express image of His person..." (He.1:3)

exceeded the concept of God held by Ahknaton for He was God in the flesh "For God so loved the world that He gave..." by which He took the initiative to resolve the problem of sin. He came to pay the price to redeem what Adam had lost to Satan through disobedience.

With reference to the concept of man, we find that the Egyptian's concept of man became the basis of Christian understanding of man as a spirit that has a soul and lives in a body. Of the three, Jesus tells us

> "It is the spirit that gives life. The flesh profits nothing" (Jn.6:63).

If it is the spirit that is of supreme importance, why would any educational system ignore it? What kind of education is possible without reference to God? How can any enlightened nation seek to allocate public funds to education while at the same time cut out any reference to God who is the source of all knowledge? The only reason behind it is that the theory of evolution that forms the philosophy of education in this country has excluded God out of the picture. With God out of our knowledge, the concept of Man is no more spirit, soul and body. Since Man is regarded as a "higher animal" with only the soul and body recognized in education, the essence of man as a spirit is excluded.

Jesus said that the truth we know sets us free from bondage. In whose interest is it that we remain in ignorance of God? Only Satan! He alone keeps everyone, including many Christians, in bondage through ignorance of the Word.

> "My people are destroyed for lack of knowledge", according to Hosea (4:6). Paul also states:
> "For the god of this world has blinded the unbelievers' minds [that they should not discern truth] preventing them from seeing the illuminating light of the Gospel of the glory of Christ (the Messiah), Who is the Image and Likeness of God" (IICor.4:4 Amplified).

Exclusion of the knowledge of God seems to me the greatest injustice to our children. It is a deliberate form of control to keep a whole generation in bondage through ignorance of the liberating Word of God. It only reminds one of the time slaves were forbidden to learn to read and write. When communist nations, like Cuba, among others, seek to control their youth from participating in the use of the Internet as recently reported, are they doing anything different? Is it not the same kind of control?

This is especially so for African-American children because they are also deprived of their African heritage through ancient Egypt which is the root of Christian faith. Prof. Asa Hilliard of George State University, makes this point clear in his introduction to the 1976 reprint of Stolen Legacy. He writes about mental bondage, with reference to the fact that much of the information exposed in that book is kept a secret from African-American students. He made reference to "the burning of the Egyptian-Ethiopian Library at Alexandria, the Inquisition, and the many book burnings in history". He asks the question: "Would Afro-American children in schools be interested in this as well as in the description of the Egyptians by the Greek Herodotus, the 'father of History,' when he described the people he saw in Egypt as 'burnt skinned, flat nosed, thick lipped and wooly haired?'"

Reference has been made to achievements including the mapping out of the Zodiac inherited by all nations. How is it that this kind of knowledge seems to be hidden and hardly taught in schools in America, especially in a context where Black children will experience pride and self-worth in a country where racism and color discrimination prevail? Could it be that this kind of knowledge is considered too liberating and empowering and as such "too dangerous", the same way that it was considered too dangerous to teach a slave to read and write? Higher self-esteem, however, has been correlated with higher achievement especially in a system where labeling is already established by one's color.

There was an experiment by a third grade teacher in the Midwest known as "Brown versus Blue eyes". This experiment was presented in a film called "The Eye of the storm". The teacher used it to teach the children about the problem of labeling and discrimination. She was able to establish that by labeling a group of them on the basis of brown or blue eyes; and constantly criticizing them; withholding praise from them, in addition to constant discouragement, they scored much lower in reading. On the other hand, the group that was encouraged, supported and rewarded with extra privileges scored much higher. When the experiment was reversed, the favored group achieved better score in their reading.

Black children need not be labeled; they already are by the color of their skin and many of them live with this kind of discouragement for life. In a chapter on "Being Black in America", in Two Nations-Black and White, Separate, Hostile, Unequal, Hacker (1992) has compellingly exposed all that black people go through in a caste system where color is the basis for privilege and exclusion. The point is the extent of the damage historically inflicted through discrimination and exclusion from privilege in addition to the fact of depriving them of such history that will lift up their self-esteem.

Teachers of other Ethnic background, regardless of their professional training, have their own prejudices and preferences. This is not limited to Whites; it is also observed among Black people from different ethnic backgrounds. However, the point is against a system where three percent African ancestry consigns one as "Black" regardless of the ninety seven percent "White" ancestry.[1] This only confirms that it is a matter of economic privilege to be allowed into this group. But even among "Christians" there is evidence of color prejudice and discrimination, and few are free of this bondage even when the knowledge of Jesus Christ is supposed to give the individual a fresh and liberating outlook on life.

It is the contention here that any kind of education that deprives children of the knowledge of God has seriously damaged and stunted the life of the individual. The student is cut off from the wealth of knowledge found in the Bible that has its deep roots in ancient Egypt. The wealth of the wisdom found in the Proverbs, for instance, has been a collection of the wisdom of the ages with their foundation in ancient Egypt. Reference has been made to proverbs ascribed to Solomon that were actually a collection from the teachings of Amen-em-ope, Pharaoh of Egypt (1405-1370 BC). Much of this has been copied word for word but that is not the point. The point is that this kind of wisdom has been gleaned over thousands of years of life experience and is an

---

1. In 1977 one Sussie G. Phipps who considered herself "white" and married white twice was defined as "black" because a 1970 Louisiana law said any one with more than 1/32nd black blood defined him as black. Ms Phipp's great-great-great-great grandmother was a black woman slave named Margarita. Ms Phipps was at least 1/32nd black (The Chronicle of Higher Education, Feb. 1995)

advice on how best to live it. When Jesus said: "I have come that you may have life, and have it more abundantly", He was saying the same thing that the Proverbs advised.

Children who had the privilege of being exposed to some of this wisdom find a new course of life charted for them. I think of one Benjamin who was having problems with a violent pathological temper. Under the grip of that temper he said: "I thrust the knife toward his belly. The knife hit his big, heavy ROTC buckle with such force that the blade snapped and dropped to the ground" (Carson with Murphy,1991). He ran home having realized that he almost killed his best friend. Because of his exposure to the Bible through his church, he locked himself in the bathroom and read from the Proverbs. He was impressed by the Prov.16:32:

> "He who is slow to anger is better than the mighty,
> And he who rules his spirit than he who takes a city."

It was this same boy who grew up to become one of America's most famous neurosurgeons, the famous Dr. Benjamin Carson. This same proverb helped this writer personally when growing up with a similar temper problem. The question is how many more children could have been helped to achieve their maximum potential to become an asset to society rather than liability languishing in jail?

Much talent has been wasted this way. In fact, Dr. Cameron in The last Pew on the Left: America's Lost potential, has laid the blame directly on the Christian church that has acquiesced "during slavery, the Reconstruction period, and even today, in matters of racism and segregation" (Cameron 1995,137). He describes racism and segregation as a "festering sore" or "cancer" and the lost potential as the "myriad of blacks who have been denied equal and fair opportunities to develop their God-given skills by making them attend "separate but equal" schools, which equality was only a myth. This was from a background of slavery where laws prohibited blacks from learning to read or write English. He points out that "the slaves were forbidden to speak in their native tongues, families were broken up, traditional customs and ties were lost, and [yet] the white man, after the Emancipation Proclamation, considered the Negro inherently dull" (ibid.,137).

But since it was false evolutionary theory that considered them "inherently dull", we have witnessed various individuals at various times who rose to excellence despite any restrictions put in their way. A few of them include Frederick Douglas, Benjamin Banneker, George W. Carver, Booker T. Washington, W.E.B DuBois, Charles Drew" among many others. Some others like Dr. Martin L. King Jr. and Malcolm X had been cut down at their prime in the process of

"fighting for the dignity and human rights constitutionally guaranteed but hypocritically denied to blacks in the society" (ibid.,138).

The tragedy is that as Nathan said to King David:

"By this deed, you have given great cause to the enemies of the Lord to blaspheme" (2 Sam.12:4).

(This was when Nathan confronted King David about his adulterous relationship with Bathsheba and the murder of Uriah at the battle front found in 2 Samuel 11-12). The Christian church has lost more potential, according to Dr. Cameron, because like David, it has "despised the commandment of the Lord to do evil in His sight" (2 Sam.12:9). The people of God are "not to be conformed to the world, but to be transformed by the renewing of their minds" (Rom.12:3), but the White church in America at large has compromised this part of God's Word regarding the evil of slavery, discrimination and segregation. The result has been discrimination, and segregated churches; and through its acquiescence, has lost much of its testimony. The Church has turned many away to seek justice and equity in other religions such

SUMMARY, CONCLUSIONS, AND SOME IMPLICATIONS 93

as Moslem because of its hypocrisy. But many also remained simply uninfluenced by the gospel and

> "there is a hopelessness in people who have not been influenced by the gospel that is extremely hard, practically impossible for the secular mind to understand" according to Dr. Cameron.

He also points out that astute observers are now beginning to recognize that

> "a large part of the problems of the increase in crime, drug addiction and the general decay of the cities, stems from racism" (ibid.,143).

Despite the weaknesses of the Church, it is still the best, if not the only hope for good in society. It was through the moral base provided by the Christian church, that Dr. Martin L. King was able to mobilize the American people to fight for equal rights. He was able to appeal to the conscience of the American people, which was formed by the principles of the Bible. This moral base has been eroded since the knowledge of God has been taken out of the schools from the 1960s. Much of the present decay and breakdown in the Public School system can be attributed to this.

Aside from that, the point is that much that is in the Bible has ancient Egyptian roots and they provide answers to life's problems because they have been founded on God's revelations and principles. Human life is of great value in the Bible and no student can take another person's life the way we experience it in schools today if they have been exposed to the teachings in the Bible. Self-esteem does not need to be taught from any other perspective than from the biblical perspective that man is created in the image of God with God's spirit in him. The problem of race and racism will be minimized as people relate to God and treat each other with love and respect, as they themselves would like to be treated. All these are denied students in American Public Schools because of a faulty philosophy of education, evolutionary theory.

As discussed earlier with reference to "the dateless past", the claim of a long earth history by the evolutionists must be conceded. How else can one account for ancient Egyptian history if the earth is only six thousand years as claimed by some Creation scientists. Similarly, there is little basis for the Evolutionists' claim of creation without divine intervention. Both concepts of God as Creator in addition to the fact of a long history of the earth have their origin in ancient Egypt, and in fact, Egyptian history cannot exist without a "dateless past" as also suggested in a book like Job which referred to the creation. In fact other books like Isaiah and Ezekiel also referred to God's perfect creation before destruction by Satan's rebellion. It was God's creation in the dateless past recorded in Job and other books of the Bible which scientists also study.

One of the consequences of denying children access to the Bible as part of their education has been a deterioration in self-discipline which translates into lower academic performance in almost every area. This is because when children and society are cut off from the light, only darkness prevails. Instead of working from the Spirit of life in Christ Jesus, they are operating from the law of sin and death, which is Satan's kingdom.

Reference has been made to the fact that African Americans students, at least, need to learn of the truth of ancient Egyptian past. Any educational philosophy seeking to really help students will never shy away from making the truth available for all to learn. If we genuinely seek to know the truth about the African past we will, but this cannot be separated from much that is also found in the Bible. This is where much of the wisdom has been deposited since the Native Africans of the Nile Valley had more experience at life and how to live it than any other groups historically. They learned early that life has to be lived with the understanding that it is not only transient but fragile; that man is created by God Almighty and that he is a spirit that has a soul

SUMMARY, CONCLUSIONS, AND SOME IMPLICATIONS

and lives in a body. The body perishes and is committed to the ground but the soul and spirit live on in eternity with God or endure punishment with Satan. The concepts of life after death and heaven and hell had their origin in ancient Egypt as seen in the Negative Confessions. "The fool has said in his heart 'There is no God'" (Ps.14:1). Only the fool can say that such concepts of heaven and hell are not real or only man's creation.

This was the perspective provided by ancient Egypt, which still continues as the perspective in the Bible. Jesus came to fulfill and expound on the laws that had been established thousands of years before the time of Abraham or Moses. As pointed out, with modern man's rejection of God in his knowledge, much truth has also been jettisoned and man has exposed himself to the lies of Satan, with devastating consequences for man's inhumanity to man. The truth is that there are not many ways leading to God. There are only two ways that had been established: the way of truth or falsehood; light or darkness; good or evil; God or Satan. Rejection of one is to expose oneself to the other. Since the days of "progressive education" by Horace Mann and John Dewey, humanism, taken from the theory of evolution, has operated on the assumption that man is sufficient to solve his own problems without reference to God.

> It is evident today that man does not have the answer. As noted above, Jeremiah stated, "It is not in man who walks to direct his own steps" (Je.10:23),

But Psalm 37:23 states:

"The steps of a good man are ordered by the Lord..."

This is because of man's bent toward sin; however much he tries, there can be only futility, which God Himself has built into the system. The problem of sin still remains. No one, independent of the Creator, can ever achieve his highest potential and the perfection that is found only in the Son, Jesus Christ. "Professing to be wise, they became fools" was Paul's judgement on those who rely on their own wisdom. He said of his fellow Jews:

> "For they being ignorant of God's righteousness, and seeking to establish their own righteousness, have not submitted to the righteousness of God" (Rom. 10:3).

Modern man refuses to submit to the righteousness of God with serious consequences. This starts at the individual human level when the truth is not taught to him as part of his basic education at the foundation level in school; he enters society and finds that there is no answer but more frustration and futility. Even when his skills learned in school or college land him a good job, the art of living has been denied him; he is skilled at how to make a living but not at how to live.

Self-discipline is a major requirement for any kind of achievement in life. Of the two ways discussed, only the way of Jesus Christ encourages self-discipline as one learns to take up one's cross and follow Jesus in obedience to the teachings in the Bible. Absence of self-discipline is one of the many consequences of being guided by a false philosophy that implies that there are no absolute standards. Absolute standards are there because God established them: both moral and spiritual just like physical laws. Any attempt to break God's standard brings destruction the same way one dares not break a physical law of gravity by jumping from a tenth floor building.

As man attempts to seek his own way and use modern scientific resources to solve his problems, he finds out that there is no easy answer. He seems to grope in the dark as one trying to find a needle in a haystack. It is because Satan is darkness and not light; he has no light in him; he is a liar and the father of lies, according to Jesus. If he has truth in him, man will find solution to his problems but he has none. Only in God is the answer. This is why any school system that purports to educate, outside of God, is only deceiving itself. The Bible says

SUMMARY, CONCLUSIONS, AND SOME IMPLICATIONS 97

that the fear of the Lord is the beginning of wisdom. There is no wisdom outside of God.

Jesus came to fulfill the plan established by the Father from the foundation of the universe. After Lucifer had been cast out of heaven and became Satan, God knew exactly what he would attempt do. Having taken dominion of the earth from Man through deception, Satan put man under his control. Jesus came to pay the price to redeem mankind but man has to use his own free will to accept or reject the free offer. To accept Jesus by faith is to be redeemed and adopted back into the kingdom of God. This means not only present life but also the assurance of life after death. Rejection of that way means the willingness to pay for the consequences of sin oneself. Even if one tried to live a perfect life we are told that all our righteousness are like filthy rags before God, according to Isaiah. This means that resources used by Christians to live this life are denied the non-Christian. Many other religions also try to establish their own righteousness, but only the one established by Jesus Christ is recognized by God the Father, who raised Him from the dead.

Jesus also said that He is coming back. He said He would come back from the dead and He did; but He also said He would come back as a judge of the whole world. On the basis of perfect fulfillment of prophecy, and also as established by the blueprint, the Zodiac, most Christians believe that this will be so. In fact, much Christian life is motivated by this positive expectation to go on and fulfill the great commission:

> "All authority has been given to Me in heaven and on earth, Go therefore and make disciples of all nations, baptizing them in the name of the Father and of the Son and of the Holy Spirit, teaching them to observe all that I have commanded you;..." (Mt.28:18-20).

One major commandment that Jesus gave His disciples was to love one another as He had loved them. Love is said to cover a multitude of sins and only in the kingdom of God, as opposed to the kingdom of Satan, do we find the expression of Christian love shown in concern for others regardless of their color, nationality or race. The positive aspects of modern civilization through education, health services, scientific developments and all the conveniences of modern life spread throughout the whole world and also came to developing countries as a result of this genuine love that enabled missionaries to sacrifice their own lives for the sake of others. It is true that some negatives also followed as Satan was also at work; but by and large, the positive has definitely outweighed the negative. Christians are still at work for their Lord spreading the gospel of the anointed Jesus. It is only His anointing that truly breaks every yoke and sets people free from the bondage of Satan.

EPILOGUE: WHEN WE SHUT OUT THE LIGHT.

"For with You is the fountain of life;
In Your light we see light" (Psalm 36:9).

When light is shut out, only darkness remains. He is the fountain of life, and He alone provides light for us to see and walk in. To shut out His light means to say "No" to Jesus Who said:

"I am the Light of the world. He who follows Me shall not walk in darkness, but have the light of life" (Jn.8:12).

Elsewhere He pointed out that light has come into the world but "men loved darkness rather than light, because their deeds were evil" (John 3:19). They fear the light because light exposes darkness but

"he who does the truth comes to the light that his deeds may be clearly seen, that they have been done in God" (Jn.3:20-21).

Could anyone deliberately shut out the light? We are told that only the enemy, Satan, blinds man's mind from seeing the light

"lest the light of the gospel of the glory of Christ, who is the image of God, should shine on them" (IICo.4:4).

It has been established in this study that there are two forces at work, God's and Satan's. To reject God means to open up oneself to the influences and destructive forces of Satan. There is no middle ground. American Public school education had been founded on a sound godly foundation. Somehow along the way, education has been derailed from this path as the truth of God has been jettisoned. As such the source of knowledge and wisdom has also been rejected. The name of Jesus cannot be mentioned in schools but there has been a wholehearted embrace of activities that invite the influence of Satan. An example is the promotion of Halloween when children's spirits are open to the enemy. All other gods can be mentioned and studied freely, but not the name of Jesus who is the "express image of God" (Heb,1:3). Even at such times as Thanksgiving, Christmas and Easter, Public School teachers cannot freely teach the truth without feeling they are going against a man-made law of "separation of Church and State". Students are therefore deprived of the most essential part of their education and thus remain in darkness. Through "Values clarification" they are supposed to choose between good and evil, right and wrong, of which they have no knowledge, since there is no knowledge of the truth of God. Moreover, they are also taught that good and evil are only relative.

Missionaries who established Christian schools in developing countries were often criticized for promoting their culture and less of those of the country's own. This may be a valid criticism where aspects of life such as clothing, food, or music unrelated to any rituals are concerned. But they were also correct in excluding aspects of native culture that were not God glorifying but rather promoted the kingdom of the enemy. For the truth is that where there is not the light of Jesus Christ, darkness prevails and all cultures that have not dealt with the problem of sin, through the shed blood of Jesus Christ, have the fabric of their culture interwoven with all works of darkness. The concept of cultural relativism implying that one culture is as good as the other, is true in the sense that since they do not recognize Jesus Christ, most of the expressions and activities of those cultures and their social fabric, will be interwoven by works of darkness. This leaves children confused. Not only do the schools promote the dubious and questionable in the culture; public education media through the TV, movies, magazines and now the Internet, promote mostly the symbols and values of the kingdom of darkness. But they do not counter-balance it with the truth of God.

The consequences for students include the feeling of hopelessness because the source of hope has been cut out. When "faith, hope and love" are shut out, the source of true power is excluded and some students seek the path of the occult and Satanism with all their dangerous and destructive consequences. God as the source of all power and authority who is available to all those who join their spirits with His Spirit, is denied access from all that He alone can do to mature the individual in knowledge, wisdom and closeness to the maturity in Jesus Christ.

Where there is no hope, there is neither meaning nor purpose in life.

A meaningless life does not see any reason for living, and sometimes suicide is viewed as a viable alternative. When one's own life is of little value, other lives do not seem to have much significance either; hence, such mass killings as we experienced in Columbine High School, aside from others which are becoming rampant of late. It is especially so, when man is not seen from God's perspective as a spirit that has a soul and lives in a body. The true worth of man is found in the sacrifice of Jesus Christ. On the contrary they are taught that man is merely a higher animal. Some even wonder why they are expected to behave differently! The youth are confused when they find out that behaving like an animal brings on consequences which they are neither aware of or prepared to accept such as in the case of aids. Just as physical laws are bound to generate cause and effect, so are moral and spiritual laws. One may be free to do what one pleases but consequences are bound to follow, and ignorance is no excuse. While students are never properly directed to understand such consequences, but are encouraged in the idea of doing what feels good, they are at the same time excluded from Christian values. Can we really claim to be educating them in the sense of fully preparing them for life when they are deprived of the source of true life? True life is found only in God through Jesus Christ. It is He, through the Holy Spirit's anointing, that can turn an ordinary life into an extraordinary one. Only He adds the "super" to the "natural" to make it supernatural.

Christianity's roots go deep down into ancient Egypt. They provided the wisdom of the ages concerning God and His Son, Jesus Christ, forever established in the heavens. Getting the best out of this life has to be moored to values that have passed the test of time. Life is only productive to the extent that it is linked to the real source of life where the Power of God, His Holy Spirit, is released to empower man to achieve his highest potential. No education outside of that truth can bring the human potential any closer to the potential God had planned for him.

REFERENCES

Asante, Molefik & Mattson, Mark T, The Historical and Cultural Atlas of African Americans, New York: Simon & Schuster MacMillan, 1992.

Banks, William D., The Heavens Declare, Kirkland, Missouri: Impact Books, 1985.

Ben-Jochannan, Yosef, Africa: Mother of Western Civilization, Baltimore: Black Classic Press, 1988.

_____, "Moses: African Influence on Judaism", In The African origins of Major World Religions, ed. Saakana, A.S., United Kingdom: Karnak House, 1988.

Budge, Wallis Sir, Egyptian Ideas of the Future Life-Egyptian Religion, New York: Bell Publishing Company, 1959 (from the 1900 Edition).

_____, The Book of the Dead; an English translation of the chapters, hymns etc. of the Theban recension, with intro, notes etc, by Sir Wallis Budge., 2nd ed. Rev. and enlarged. New York: Barnes and Nobles, inc. 1951.

Cameron, Robert J., The Last Pew on the Left: America's Lost Potential, Los Angeles: Prescott Press, Inc. 1995.

Carr-Harris, Bertha, The Hieroglyphics of the Heavens, Toronto: Armac Press, 1933.

Carson, B. with Cecil Murphy, Gifted Hands—The Ben Carson story, Grand Rapids: Zondervan Publishing House, 1991.

Church, F. Leslie, ed. The NIV Matthew Henry Commentary in One Volume, Based on the Broad Oak Edition, Revising ed., G.W. Peterson, Grand Rapids: Zondervan Publishing House, 1992.

Count A de Gobineau, "Essays on the Inequality of the Human races", In The Study of Man, ed. Linton, Ralph, New York: Appleton-Century-Crafts Inc.,1936.

Finch, Charles S., "The Kamitic Genesis of Christianity",In The African Origins of Major World Religions, ed. Saakana, A.S., United Kingdom: Karnak House, 1988.

Fleming, Kenneth C., God's Voice in the Stars: Zodiac Signs and Bible Truth, Neptune, New Jersey, 1981.

Hacker, Andrew, Two Nations: Black and White, Separate, Hostile, Unequal. New York: Random House,1992

Hinckley, K.C., A Compact Guide to the Christian Life, Compiled by Navpress: Colorado Springs, 1993.

Hinn, Benny, Lord, I need a Miracle, Nashville: Thomas Nelson Publishers, 1993.

James,George G.M. Stolen Legacy: The Greeks were not the authors of Greek Philosophy, but the people of North Africa, commonly called the Egyptians. Intro to 1988 Reprint & Biographical notes on George GM James by Asa G. Hilliard:San Francisco:Julian Richardson Associates,1988.

Johnson, Phillip, An Easy-To-Understand Guide for Defeating Darwinism by Opening Minds, Downers Grove: Intervasity Press, 1997.

Kennedy, D.James, The Real Meaning of the Zodiac., Compiled and edited by Nancy Britt, from a series of sermons on the Zodiac by D.James Kennedy, Fort Lauderdale: CRM Publishing, 1989.

Klineberg, Otto, Race Differences, New York: Harper and Brothers, 1935.

Morris, Henry M., Many Infallible Proofs, San Diego: Creation-Life Publishers, 1974.

Ofiaja, Nicholas, "Colonial Division of Africa: The Harbinger of the two World Wars," African Personality Magazine, Vol. 5 No.2, 2000.

Payne, Elizabeth, The Pharaohs of Ancient Egypt, New York: Random House, 1964.

Guideposts Parallel Bible: King James Version, Modern Language Bible, Living Bible, Revised Standard Version, Grand Rapids: Zondervan Corporation, 1973.

Ritzer, George, Modern Sociological Theory, New York: The McGraw Hill Companies, 1996.Seiss, Joseph A., The Gospel in the Stars, Grand Rapids: Castel Press,1979.

Wetteran, Bruce, World History: A dictionary of Important People, Places, and Events, from Ancient Times to the present, New York: Henry Holt & Company, 1994.

About the Author

Dr. Ocansey was raised in Ghana, W. A. He received his B.A (Ed.) from the University of Ghana, a double Masters and Ph.D. from Columbia University. He has been in Education for over thirty years, with over twenty in NYC Public schools. He is currently an Adjunct Professor at the College of New Rochelle.

0-595-21474-6

Printed in the United Kingdom
by Lightning Source UK Ltd.
105320UKS00002B/77

9 780595 214747